TOEIC

練習測驗（11）

聽力錄音QR碼（1~100題）

LISTENING TEST

In the Listening test, you will be asked to demonstrate how well you understand spoken English. The entire Listening test will last approximately 45 minutes. There are four parts, and directions are given for each part. You must mark your answers on the separate answer sheet. Do not write your answers in your test book.

PART 1

Directions: For each question in this part, you will hear four statements about a picture in your test book. When you hear the statements, you must select the one statement that best describes what you see in the picture. Then find the number of the question on your answer sheet and mark your answer. The statements will not be printed in your test book and will be spoken only one time.

Statement (C), "They're sitting at a table," is the best description of the picture, so you should select answer (C) and mark it on your answer sheet.

1.

2.

GO ON TO THE NEXT PAGE.

3.

4.

5.

6.

GO ON TO THE NEXT PAGE.

Directions: You will hear a question or statement and three responses spoken in English. They will not be printed in your test book and will be spoken only one time. Select the best response to the question or statement and mark the letter (A), (B), or (C) on your answer sheet.

7. Mark your answer on your answer sheet.

8. Mark your answer on your answer sheet.

9. Mark your answer on your answer sheet.

10. Mark your answer on your answer sheet.

11. Mark your answer on your answer sheet.

12. Mark your answer on your answer sheet.

13. Mark your answer on your answer sheet.

14. Mark your answer on your answer sheet.

15. Mark your answer on your answer sheet.

16. Mark your answer on your answer sheet.

17. Mark your answer on your answer sheet.

18. Mark your answer on your answer sheet.

19. Mark your answer on your answer sheet.

20. Mark your answer on your answer sheet.

21. Mark your answer on your answer sheet.

22. Mark your answer on your answer sheet.

23. Mark your answer on your answer sheet.

24. Mark your answer on your answer sheet.

25. Mark your answer on your answer sheet.

26. Mark your answer on your answer sheet.

27. Mark your answer on your answer sheet.

28. Mark your answer on your answer sheet.

29. Mark your answer on your answer sheet.

30. Mark your answer on your answer sheet.

31. Mark your answer on your answer sheet.

Directions: You will hear some conversations between two people. You will be asked to answer three questions about what the speakers say in each conversation. Select the best response to each question and mark the letter (A), (B), (C), or (D) on your answer sheet. The conversation will not be printed in your test book and will be spoken only one time.

32. What are the speakers discussing?
(A) A presentation.
(B) A television show.
(C) A website.
(D) A bank loan.

33. What does the man say he is missing?
(A) A signature.
(B) A video clip.
(C) A password.
(D) An e-mail address.

34. What does the man say he will do after lunch?
(A) Contact a journalist.
(B) Review some data.
(C) Check a computer.
(D) Write a proposal.

35. Why did the woman stop by City Hall?
(A) To claim a lost item.
(B) To speak with an administrator.
(C) To register for an event.
(D) To file for a permit.

36. Where is the woman instructed to go?
(A) To a local park.
(B) To the courthouse.
(C) To a department store.
(D) To a community center.

37. What does the woman ask for?
(A) Some updated flyers.
(B) A building directory.
(C) A map of the city.
(D) A list of cleaning companies.

38. Why is the woman calling?
(A) To answer a question.
(B) To report an incorrect charge.
(C) To close an account.
(D) To ask about a policy.

39. What is the woman also concerned about?
(A) Frequent flyer miles.
(B) Membership fees.
(C) Interest rates.
(D) Identity theft.

40. What does the man ask for?
(A) A payment date.
(B) A street address.
(C) An account number.
(D) A password.

41. What is the conversation mainly about?
(A) A website.
(B) A sales report.
(C) A budget review.
(D) A job interview.

42. What does the man want to do?
(A) Implement a new hiring policy.
(B) Begin a renovation project.
(C) Implement an advertising campaign.
(D) Discuss an idea.

43. What does the man say he will do before the meeting?
(A) Read a resume.
(B) Hire a programmer.
(C) Print some flyers.
(D) Revise a concept.

GO ON TO THE NEXT PAGE.

44. What does the man want the woman to do?
    (A) Have lunch with a client.
    (B) Lead a training session.
    (C) Stay late.
    (D) Work from home.

45. What does the woman suggest?
    (A) Switching offices.
    (B) Taking a later flight.
    (C) Canceling a meeting.
    (D) Asking a co-worker.

46. When is the conversation most likely taking place?
    (A) On Monday.
    (B) On Thursday.
    (C) On Friday.
    (D) On Saturday.

47. Why is the man calling?
    (A) To obtain a document.
    (B) To ask about a moving service.
    (C) To check on an order.
    (D) To report a lost key.

48. What does the woman suggest that the man do?
    (A) Send her an e-mail.
    (B) Come to her office.
    (C) Bring a copy of an invoice.
    (D) Speak with the maintenance department.

49. What does the man ask about?
    (A) Changing a schedule.
    (B) Finding an office location.
    (C) Selecting a moving date.
    (D) Making a duplicate key.

50. What area does the man work in?
    (A) Personnel.
    (B) Engineering.
    (C) Sales.
    (D) Advertising.

51. What surprised the man about his new position?
    (A) The amount of paperwork.
    (B) The speed of the network.
    (C) The frequency of travel.
    (D) The long hours.

52. What has the company done recently?
    (A) Upgraded a system.
    (B) Discontinued a product.
    (C) Launched a marketing campaign.
    (D) Hired new employees.

53. Where does the man work?
    (A) At a bank.
    (B) At a furniture store.
    (C) At a post office.
    (D) At a news organization.

54. Why is the man contacting the woman?
    (A) A new credit card will be issued.
    (B) A transaction has been reversed.
    (C) A delivery was sent to a wrong address.
    (D) A large amount was charged to her account.

55. What did the woman most likely do?
    (A) Make a complaint.
    (B) Buy some furniture.
    (C) Lose her mobile phone.
    (D) Take out a loan.

56. What event are the speakers discussing?
(A) A banquet.
(B) A wedding.
(C) A business trip.
(D) A client.

57. What does the man say about the restaurant?
(A) Service is slow.
(B) The menu needs revision.
(C) The food is very good.
(D) Seating is limited.

58. What does the woman imply?
(A) She doesn't have enough time to finish her work.
(B) Many employees can't attend the event.
(C) The banquet is not important.
(D) Her budget is unlimited.

59. Where is the conversation taking place?
(A) At a park.
(B) At a café.
(C) At a furniture store.
(D) At a supermarket.

60. What does Louisa suggest that the man do?
(A) Open a window.
(B) Use a coupon.
(C) Visit a plant shop.
(D) Extend business hours.

61. What does the man ask Louisa for?
(A) A list of prices.
(B) A deadline extension.
(C) Some coffee.
(D) Some photographs.

Company	Location
Avatar Studios	Columbus
Taylor & Martin	Columbus
Buckeye Silk Screen Co.	Cleveland
Icon Graphic	Cincinnati

62. What is the company sponsoring?
(A) A pancake breakfast.
(B) A charity run.
(C) A golf outing.
(D) A weekend retreat.

63. What is the man concerned about?
(A) A limited budget.
(B) A weather forecast.
(C) A safety issue.
(D) An ad campaign.

64. Look at the graphic. Which company do the speakers choose?
(A) Avatar Studios
(B) Buckeye Silk Screen Co.
(C) Icon Design
(D) Taylor & Martin

GO ON TO THE NEXT PAGE.

DIRECTORY

Unger Fertility Clinic	Suite 101
Dr. Karl Edwards, OB-GYN	Suite 110
Smithson Cosmetic Surgery	Suite 201
Kreutz Eye Care	Suite 210
Weiner & Associates	Suite 301

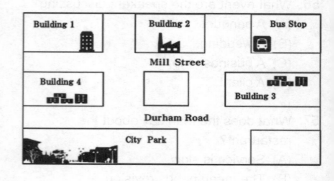

65. What is the purpose of the woman's visit?
(A) To have her car serviced.
(B) To deliver a package.
(C) To see a doctor.
(D) To attend a seminar.

66. What can the man do for the woman?
(A) Validate her parking.
(B) Reschedule her appointment.
(C) Park her car.
(D) Issue a rain check.

67. Look at the graphic. Which office name has to be updated on the building directory?
(A) Unger Fertility Clinic
(B) Kreutz Eye Care
(C) Dr. Karl Edwards, OB-GYN
(D) Smithson Cosmetic Surgery

68. Who most likely is the woman?
(A) A postal worker.
(B) A delivery driver.
(C) A repair technician.
(D) A building manager.

69. What problem does the woman mention?
(A) A package has been damaged.
(B) A vehicle is not working.
(C) Some residents are not home.
(D) Some information is missing.

70. Look at the graphic. Where will the woman go next?
(A) To building 1.
(B) To building 2.
(C) To building 3.
(D) To building 4.

PART 4

Directions: You will hear some talks given by a single speaker. You will be asked to answer three questions about what the speaker says in each talk. Select the best response to each question and mark the letter (A), (B), (C), or (D) on your answer sheet. The talks will not be printed in your test book and will be spoken only one time.

71. What is the purpose of the message?
 (A) To arrange a meeting.
 (B) To confirm an order.
 (C) To apply for a job.
 (D) To make a reservation.

72. What does the speaker imply when he says, //"Can you believe the grand opening is less than a month away?"//?
 (A) Projects will be completed on time.
 (B) Decisions must be made quickly.
 (C) Appointments must be rescheduled.
 (D) Reservations will be hard to get.

73. What will the speaker most likely do after Nina replies?
 (A) E-mail some documents.
 (B) Make some phone calls.
 (C) Fill out an application.
 (D) Hire a manager.

74. What is the talk mainly about?
 (A) Planning an annual celebration.
 (B) Analyzing traffic patterns.
 (C) Attracting visitors to a park.
 (D) Building a wildlife refuge.

75. What problem does the speaker mention?
 (A) Scheduling conflicts.
 (B) Insufficient funding.
 (C) Zoning laws.
 (D) Broken equipment.

76. What are listeners asked to do?
 (A) Make a list of business owners.
 (B) Volunteer for a project.
 (C) Donate some money.
 (D) Choose a location.

77. What service is being advertised?
 (A) Computer consulting.
 (B) Overnight delivery.
 (C) A training course.
 (D) A recycling program.

78. How can listeners receive a discount?
 (A) By completing a survey.
 (B) By visiting the website.
 (C) By recycling an electronic device.
 (D) By entering a lottery.

79. What does the speaker say can be found on a website?
 (A) Recycling information.
 (B) Discount vouchers.
 (C) Instructional videos.
 (D) Store locations.

80. Where is the announcement being made?
 (A) At a shopping mall.
 (B) At an airport.
 (C) At a bus terminal.
 (D) At a train station.

81. What does the speaker ask listeners to do?
 (A) Return at a later time.
 (B) Go to the customer service desk.
 (C) Apply for a refund.
 (D) Contact another airline.

82. According to the speaker, what will be distributed?
 (A) Headphones.
 (B) Reading materials.
 (C) Hotel vouchers.
 (D) Refreshments.

GO ON TO THE NEXT PAGE.

83. What is the main topic of the meeting?
   (A) A competitor's products.
   (B) An instructional video.
   (C) Survey results.
   (D) An online review.

84. What feature of the product does the speaker mention?
   (A) Remote control.
   (B) Color options.
   (C) Durability.
   (D) Easier cleaning.

85. What does the speaker imply when he says, //"the user's manual is currently about 10 pages too long"//?
   (A) Pages will be added to the manual.
   (B) The manual will be shortened.
   (C) The manual is available to download online.
   (D) Customers should read the manual thoroughly.

86. What type of business does the speaker work for?
   (A) An employment agency.
   (B) A fitness center.
   (C) An advertising firm.
   (D) A shipping company.

87. What does the speaker imply by, //"standing-room only"//?
   (A) He is pointing out that the office will close soon.
   (B) He recommends that a project date be extended.
   (C) Some seats are still available.
   (D) The room is very crowded.

88. What does the speaker ask the listeners to do?
   (A) Make a copy of their identification.
   (B) Complete some paperwork.
   (C) Stand at attention.
   (D) Confirm their contact information.

89. Where do the listeners work?
   (A) At a brokerage firm.
   (B) At an art gallery.
   (C) At a medical clinic.
   (D) At a hair salon.

90. What will the listeners be doing today?
   (A) Making trades.
   (B) Attending a seminar.
   (C) Distributing flyers.
   (D) Watching a film.

91. What has the speaker done for the listeners?
   (A) Decorated an office.
   (B) Marked locations on a map.
   (C) Written recommendation letters.
   (D) Provided theater tickets.

92. What kind of business does the speaker work for?
   (A) A local jeweler.
   (B) A public relations agency.
   (C) A department store.
   (D) An architectural firm.

93. What is the speaker announcing?
   (A) A new partnership.
   (B) A groundbreaking ceremony.
   (C) An employee promotion.
   (D) An award nomination.

94. What does the speaker say about Greg Stiles's project?
   (A) It promoted collaboration across departments.
   (B) It led to changes to a company policy.
   (C) It attracted interest from competing firms.
   (D) It made use of eco-friendly materials.

ORDER FORM

Item	Quantity
Inkjet cartridges (B&W)	10
Time cards (50 ct.)	2
Post-It notes (100 ct.)	200
Coffee filters (10 ct.)	4

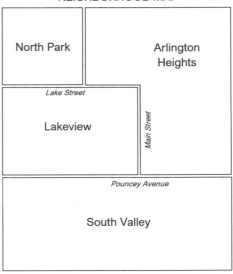

NEIGHBORHOOD MAP

95. Look at the graphic. Which quantity on the order form will be changed?
(A) 2.
(B) 4.
(C) 10.
(D) 200.

96. What did the speaker say she did?
(A) Adjusted the quantity of an order.
(B) Gave a product demonstration.
(C) Inspected a facility.
(D) Went on vacation.

97. What does the speaker say about Terry Finch?
(A) He will be training a new employee.
(B) He will be taking care of some accounts.
(C) He will deliver the shipment.
(D) He will maintain the website.

98. What type of business does the speaker own?
(A) A chain of restaurants.
(B) A flower shop.
(C) A taxi service.
(D) A local grocery store.

99. Look at the graphic. In which neighborhood does the speaker want to offer a new service?
(A) North Park
(B) Lakeview
(C) Arlington Heights
(D) South Valley

100. What does the speaker want to discuss next?
(A) An updated vacation policy.
(B) A renovation project.
(C) Advertising strategies.
(D) Hiring procedures.

This is the end of the Listening test. Turn to Part 5 in your test book.

GO ON TO THE NEXT PAGE.

READING TEST

In the Reading test, you will read a variety of texts and answer several different types of reading comprehension questions. The entire Reading test will last 75 minutes. There are three parts, and directions are given for each part. You are encouraged to answer as many questions as possible within the time allowed.

You must mark your answers on the separate answer sheet. Do not write your answers in your test book.

PART 5

Directions: A word or phrase is missing in each of the sentences below. Four answer choices are given below each sentence. Select the best answer to complete the sentence. Then mark the letter (A), (B), (C), or (D) on your answer sheet.

101. The summer concert series at Marshall Arena in Chicago is already ------- sold out.
(A) complete
(B) completed
(C) completely
(D) completion

102. Galaxy Custom Print Shop offers numerous options for ------- full-service and do-it-yourself document processing.
(A) few
(B) both
(C) many
(D) neither

103. The Throckmorton Sculpture Gardens will be ------- to the public from early spring to late autumn.
(A) open
(B) grown
(C) noticed
(D) entered

104. Spokane House Plans Inc. is looking for an ------- to coordinate multi-family housing projects.
(A) architecture
(B) architecturally
(C) architectural
(D) architect

105. Be sure to speak ------- into the microphone for the duration of your speech.
(A) probably
(B) briefly
(C) directly
(D) finally

106. Next month, Mr. Swank, our graphic designer, ------- his new designs for the company logo.
(A) exhibiting
(B) will exhibit
(C) exhibited
(D) has exhibited

107. Potential consumers have expressed great ------- in the new line of trucks from Rodeo Motors.
(A) benefit
(B) interest
(C) attention
(D) advantage

108. Survey results show that a ------- of consumers would like a wider variety of locally-sourced and organic produce.
(A) point
(B) complaint
(C) majority
(D) summary

109. Construction will not begin on the new escalator near the Houston Street subway entrance ------- next week.
(A) behind
(B) since
(C) until
(D) in

110. First Data Corporation, an ------- Atlanta-based company, assists its new employees with relocation expenses.
(A) established
(B) establish
(C) establishing
(D) establishes

111. After ------- reviewed the documents, please sign the approval form.
(A) you've
(B) your
(C) yours
(D) yourself

112. ------- employee benefits, Chasen-Hoff Biometrics offers a generous amount of vacation time.
(A) For example
(B) In terms of
(C) Because
(D) Whereas

113. The town of Downers Grove is ------- bids from local companies to build a new picnic area at Maple Lake Park.
(A) proceeding
(B) competing
(C) electing
(D) accepting

114. Although the research project has been approved, it is still not ------- clear how will be funded.
(A) perfected
(B) perfect
(C) perfectly
(D) perfection

115. Smoking, eating and drinking are ------- forbidden in the theater.
(A) strict
(B) strictly
(C) strictest
(D) stricter

116. ------- of the construction work on the Hamilton Skyway will be performed at night to minimize the traffic congestion.
(A) Already
(B) Usually
(C) Most
(D) Almost

117. Visitors must refrain ------- using flash photography inside the museum's French impressionism exhibit.
(A) with
(B) among
(C) through
(D) from

118. Failure to comply with the rules ------- on this list will result in the loss of computer lab privileges.
(A) outlined
(B) outlines
(C) outlining
(D) outline

119. Fulcrum International Holdings has agreed to buy Vandersloot Logistics in a deal ------- up to two billion dollars.
(A) except
(B) together with
(C) worth
(D) on account of

120. Ms. Bettencourt has requested that ------- related to the upcoming relocation be reported separately.
(A) expenses
(B) expensively
(C) expensive
(D) expensed

GO ON TO THE NEXT PAGE.

121. Due to hazardous weather conditions, the outdoor dinner to benefit Pine Ridge Children's hospital has been ------- until August 3.
(A) programmed
(B) defined
(C) classified
(D) postponed

122. Ascott CEO Carly Kittson claimed that creating the partnership with Morton Manufacturing is her ------- accomplishment.
(A) gratify
(B) more gratified
(C) most gratifying
(D) gratifyingly

123. Road Rage Automotive is a trusted brand with a ------- for developing innovative products and supporting them with outstanding customer service.
(A) confirmation
(B) caption
(C) reputation
(D) recognition

124. As managing editor, Elizabeth Hankey ensures that technical manuals are written in ------- language that the general public can understand.
(A) plain
(B) plainest
(C) plainly
(D) plainness

125. ------- nutritional information for our energy drinks is available on our website.
(A) Detailing
(B) Detailed
(C) Detail
(D) Details

126. Dennis Everton, service manager of Northwest Car Center, is overseeing ------- with auto-glass suppliers in the Brookfield area.
(A) negotiate
(B) negotiates
(C) negotiations
(D) negotiated

127. Consumer advocates in Saudi Arabia have ------- concern about proposed Internet regulations.
(A) focused
(B) appeared
(C) applied
(D) expressed

128. ------- other year, Johnson Motors Inc., conducts a customer-satisfaction survey to determine how warranty services can be improved.
(A) During
(B) Only
(C) About
(D) Every

129. Live seafood such as lobsters and crabs must be shipped in a ------- that does not expose them to extreme temperatures.
(A) type
(B) behavior
(C) manner
(D) purpose

130. Lee Yuan Mining Group is expected to ------- the planned expansion of its rare earths excavation in Kenya during the press briefing on Wednesday.
(A) announce
(B) organize
(C) reflect
(D) suppose

PART 6

Directions: Read the texts that follow. A word, phrase, or sentence is missing in parts of each text. Four answer choices are given below each of the texts. Select the best answer to complete the text. Then mark the letter (A), (B), (C), or (D) on your answer sheet.

Questions 131-134 refer to the following e-mail.

| To: Trent Hong |
| From: Veronica Carson |
| Date: May 4 |
| Subject: Monroe City |

Dear Trent,

I was recently informed of your upcoming ------- to the Monroe City office.
131.

As you ------- for the big move, I want to wish you the best and offer my
132.

assistance. I'm familiar with the ------- you'll face during the transition.
133.

So don't hesitate to contact me if you need any help.

-------.
134.

Best wishes,
Veronica Carson

---

131. (A) award
(B) introduction
(C) transfer
(D) event

132. (A) prepare
(B) prepared
(C) preparing
(D) have prepared

133. (A) challenging
(B) challenged
(C) challenger
(D) challenges

134. (A) What's more, the Monroe City office is larger and has more parking
(B) Otherwise, the management team is considering your proposal
(C) In the meantime, I have no doubt that you will succeed in your new role
(D) Nevertheless, I have chosen to accept this relocation

GO ON TO THE NEXT PAGE.

Top Restaurant Shakes Up the Industry

SONOMA — Renowned eatery El Dorado Kitchen is making

national ------- by putting a 'no tipping' policy in effect. The
    135.

restaurant has 'No Tipping' signs posted ------- its facility, and
                             136.

when customers pay by credit card, there is no option to

leave a tip on the order receipt. The restaurant's research

showed that over 80% of customers like the policy because it

takes away the need for math at the end of a -------. Owner
                 137.

and head chef Bob Conway revealed in an interview that he's

been inundated with positive reviews. -------.
         138.

135. (A) monuments
    (B) footnotes
    (C) titles
    (D) headlines

136. (A) among
    (B) throughout
    (C) above
    (D) upon

137. (A) ride
    (B) meal
    (C) rehearsal
    (D) complaint

138. (A) Now, other popular restaurants in the area are considering a similar policy change in the upcoming months
    (B) One of the big problems with tipping is that it's obviously unfair, and smart servers have figured out how to cheat the system
    (C) Restaurants give up a significant tax credit by eliminating tips, and the potential effect on menu prices is uncertain
    (D) A recent study indicates cutting tips could actually hurt servers, and El Dorado has significantly scaled back its trial run

Annette Shapiris
9900 Ventura Boulevard
Sherman Oaks, CA 90031

Dear Ms. Shapiris,

Your records ------- that you have dental conditions that are still untreated.
      139.
During your dental exam on April 12, these problems were noted:

- Decay on teeth #3, 14, 15, 31
- Abscess on tooth #31

- Broken tooth #19
- Gum disease

-------.
140.

Please contact us to schedule your appointments to treat these dental problems
before they progress -------. We are happy to review your treatment plan if you
      141.
would like. If it has been more than three months since your exam, you might
need a new exam in order to reevaluate your problems and update your -------
      142.
treatment.

Sincerely,
Farquar Niles & Associates, DDS

139. (A) process
(B) indicate
(C) explain
(D) examine

140. (A) The schedule fills up quicker as the end of the year approaches
(B) Your tooth has been prepared for a new crown
(C) We will gladly return the enclosed authorization with their name and address
(D) Delaying treatment of these problems will only result in further damage

141. (A) farther
(B) further
(C) furthest
(D) furthermore

142. (A) apprehensive
(B) recommended
(C) complimentary
(D) unusual

GO ON TO THE NEXT PAGE.

Infoaxis, an IT solutions and ------- company, has announced an
143.
office relocation and expansion. The New Jersey-based firm
has moved its offices from Allendale to downtown Newark. The
move stems from Infoaxis' need for ------- space to accommodate
144.
growth in demand for the firm's services. The company has
more than doubled its square footage with the move. -------.
145.

"We have seen our growth accelerate over recent years, and our
new location and facilities will allow us to continue enhancing
our ability to serve our customers ------- the highest levels," says
146.
Infoaxis' co-founder and President Gabi Haberfeld.

The new facility is equipped with a high-tech corporate briefing
room and a new state-of-the-art Data Center.

143. (A) services
(B) location
(C) partner
(D) exercise

144. (A) additional
(B) optional
(C) conditional
(D) seasonal

145. (A) Undetected faults are the primary contributor to low reliability and high maintenance in aircraft wiring
(B) Infoaxis has a significant presence in Massachusetts, with nearly 5,000 employees across the state
(C) At 14,000 square feet, the building gives Infoaxis the opportunity for massive expansion
(D) Since 1999, Infoaxis has helped business owners get a real return on their technology investments

146. (A) in
(B) for
(C) of
(D) at

Directions: In this part you will read a selection of texts, such as magazine and newspaper articles, e-mails, and instant messages. Each text or set of texts is followed by several questions. Select the best answer for each question and mark the letter (A), (B), (C), or (D) on your answer sheet.

Questions 147-148 refer to the following notice.

PUBLIC NOTICE

The Huntsville Ombudsman is holding its annual Huntsville Metro Recycling Day on Saturday, August 31, between 8:00 a.m. and 6:00 p.m. at Juanita Castro Park. This is an opportunity for local residents to dispose of items they no longer use, including appliances, furniture, and electronic devices such as computer equipment. Items will be sold in a community sale or recycled when possible. Please make sure that personal information has been deleted from donated electronic equipment. All proceeds from the sale of donated items support the "Keep Huntsville Clean" project. Don't miss the opportunity to do some spring cleaning and help our local environment.

Do you want to donate something that won't fit in your car? We will be happy to send a truck to pick it up for you. Call D'Andre Flint at 909-5126 to make arrangements. Volunteers are needed to help sort donations. To volunteer, call Niko Variakis at 909-5122.

---

147. What are Huntsville residents asked to do?
(A) Review a local recycling policy.
(B) Update their computer equipment.
(C) Donate unwanted items.
(D) Provide personal information.

148. Why should residents call Mr. Flint?
(A) To volunteer to drive a truck.
(B) To subscribe to the Huntsville Ombudsman.
(C) To make reservations at Juanita Castro Park.
(D) To request help transporting an item.

GO ON TO THE NEXT PAGE.

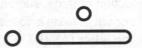

To: Kim Shelby
From: North Pacific Airlines Passenger Services
Time/Date: April 15, 12:40 P.M.

MESSAGE ALERT: See below for schedule changes for North Pacific Airlines Flight 7G600

Flight 7G600 Osaka International Airport (ITM) to Taoyuan (Taiwan) International Airport (TPE)

DELAYED

Scheduled departure 4:15 P.M.
Actual departure 5:30 P.M.
Estimated arrival at TPE: 8:15 P.M.
Departure gate: To be announced
Baggage claim: Carousel 4

If you have a connecting flight, please check with our ground service crew for transfer information.

149. Why was the text message sent?
  (A) To inform a passenger of a cancellation.
  (B) To confirm a ticket purchase.
  (C) To announce a change in flight status.
  (D) To provide an update about lost baggage.

150. What is indicated about Ms. Shelby?
  (A) She missed a connecting flight.
  (B) She will depart from Osaka.
  (C) She checked two bags onto a flight.
  (D) She paid for her flight in Taiwan.

Replanting and Maintenance

When plants are transferred to new locations, special care is required to ensure that they arrive safely and thrive in their new environment. Carry all plants by their containers (or root ball), as carrying them by their tops or trunks may damage the roots. Follow the watering guidelines in the directions-for-care pamphlet for the specific type of plant you have purchased. These pamphlets are available free of charge and are located near the checkout registers.

151. For whom is the information primarily intended?
(A) Safety inspectors.
(B) Store managers.
(C) People selling containers.
(D) People purchasing plants.

152. What is available at no cost?
(A) Boxes.
(B) Delivery.
(C) Seed packets.
(D) Written instructions

GO ON TO THE NEXT PAGE.

Please Join Us!

What: The Sea at Dusk: The world-premiere production of noted playwright Oliver Kimball's latest work.

Where: Cavalier Performing Arts Center, Roanoke

When: Saturday, October 12. Bus leaves employee parking area at 9:00 a.m.

Estimated return time: 10:00 P.M.

Cost: $65.00 per person for round-trip transportation, lunch, and admission to the 2:00 p.m. matinee performance. Money will be collected upon boarding the bus During the return trip, we'll make a **brief** stop at the Roanoke Galleria, where you may purchase dinner or a snack if you wish.

Note: To participate, you must sign up in advance on the sign-up sheet in the upstairs break room. The sheet will be **posted** until 5:00 p.m. on October 5. These excursions fill up quickly, so act soon.

For more information, please contact Gabby Susskind at the reception desk (extension 24, or e-mail: gabby@grantland.com)

153. What type of event is being publicized?
(A) A sightseeing tour.
(B) A shopping excursion.
(C) A beach trip.
(D) A theater outing.

154. Where should participants submit payment for the event?
(A) At the Cavalier Performing Arts Center.
(B) In the upstairs break room.
(C) At the reception desk.
(D) On the bus.

Planning your next travel experience?
Look no further than Ubertrek International!!

Ubertrek International now offers new vacation packages to an even wider variety of destinations. We have recently partnered with major hotel chains in the world and can offer the best deal in the best locations. New options added for the summer season include:

Sicilian Nights: Spend 6 days and 5 nights on the beautiful Mediterranean Sea aboard the San Giuseppe cruise ship. The ship will dock for special day trips in Palermo, Messina, Syracuse and Marsala.

Grecian Exploration: Tour famous Greek isles. The 10-day, 9-night tour will include visits to Santorini, Argos, Crete, and Mykonos. Package includes airfares, transportation between cities, and hotel stays.

South American Adventure: Explore the wonders of South America on this exclusive 2-week trip. Professor Carlos Enrique, a well-known expert on the history of the region will lead travelers on a tour of the Amazon River and modern Brazil. At the same time, travelers will enjoy the beautiful landscapes, unique culture, and exciting foods of the region. Package include airfares, hotel stays, train fares, and bus transportation.

In addition to these options, Ubertrek continues to offer customers assistance in booking flights and renting automobiles.

155. What has changed at Ubertrek International?
(A) New vacation options have been made.
(B) Additional tour agents have been hired.
(C) Prices on vacation packages have been reduced.
(D) A new office has been opened.

156. Who is Carlos Enrique?
(A) A chef.
(B) A historian.
(C) A landscape designer.
(D) A ship's captain.

157. What is NOT stated about Ubertrek International?
(A) It collaborates with hotel chains.
(B) It helps people reserve rental cars.
(C) It guarantees the lowest rates on air trips.
(D) It offers special options for summer vacation.

GO ON TO THE NEXT PAGE.

Cambridge Medical Associates
67 Edgewater Road
Milwaukee, Wisconsin 65711
September 2

Dear Great Lakes Supply:

In my search for a new supplier, I was referred to your company by a colleague of mine from the Banyan Pharmaceutical Group. He indicated that he has been purchasing supplies from you for more than five years, and after I had mentioned some of the problems I had been having with another vendor, he emphasized your customer service and personable staff.

In fact, I've already found what he said to be true. When I tried to place an order online, I kept getting an error message after clicking the "Submit" button at the end of the form. I telephoned the customer service number, and the representative, Tiffany, explained that there was a temporary problem with the website. Because I was in a rush to get these supplies, she advised me to fax my request instead of mailing it or waiting for the website to come back online. I was surprised by how patiently Tiffany walked me through the steps for finding and printing the order form. I readily completed it and am now sending it as suggested, along with this brief feedback.

Despite initial displeasure over the ordering problem, I was quite pleased by my first interaction with your staff, and I look forward to receiving my first order from your company. Thanks again.

Sincerely,
Consuelo Pineda
Cambridge Medical Associates

158. What is suggested about Great Lakes Supply?
(A) It specializes in selling office machines.
(B) Its customer service representatives request feedback.
(C) Its website has been unavailable for over a week.
(D) It has been in business for at least five years.

159. What is implied about Ms. Pineda's previous supplier?
(A) Its prices were too high.
(B) Its delivery times were unreasonable.
(C) Its website was difficult to use.
(D) Its customer service was poor.

160. How did Ms. Pineda submit her order to Great Lakes Supply?
(A) By postal mail.
(B) By e-mail.
(C) By fax.
(D) By telephone.

From:	Bryant Southern <generalmanager@lacarmela.com.ph>
To:	All staff members <mailing_list@lacarmela.com.ph>
Re:	Employee of the Month
Date:	June 3

Last week, resort owner Hiram Peretz announced his new Employee of the Month program. This program will recognize full-time employees who show an outstanding commitment to serving La Carmela Resort Boracay. Examples of exceptional work include saving the resort money, meeting a difficult deadline, or serving guests in a way that exceeds usual duties.

Nominations may be submitted by any La Carmela Resort Boracay guest or employee. Forms are available at the concierge desk and can also be printed from our website. Nominations for this month are due by June 21. A special box for completed forms has been placed next to the front door. Managers will review the nominations and select the winner during their monthly planning meeting.

La Carmela Resort Boracay employees of the month will receive a monetary award, a certificate of appreciation signed by Mr. Peretz, and an invitation to an annual employee-recognition dinner. We believe that this will be a wonderful opportunity to recognize our hard-working and dedicated employees!

Sincerely,
The Management

161. Where are nomination forms submitted?
    (A) By the main entrance.
    (B) At the concierge desk.
    (C) In the manager's office.
    (D) On the hotel website.

162. What is indicated about award recipients?
    (A) They have worked at the hotel for at least one year.
    (B) They will receive money as part of the award.
    (C) They may bring a guest to the employee-recognition dinner.
    (D) They will be selected on July 1.

163. What is stated about the resort owner?
    (A) He sent the e-mail to everyone in the company.
    (B) He will sign certificates of appreciation.
    (C) He meets with managers on a monthly basis.
    (D) He knows all his employees by name.

GO ON TO THE NEXT PAGE.

Trade Commission Projections Now Available

October 1 — The Edwardsville Trade Commission has released its latest Regional Labor Forecast. – 1 –. The report provides information about the fastest growing industries and occupations as well as those in decline. The report is released biannually, in April and October, to ensure the data reflect the current labor market in Edwardsville and the surrounding region. – 2 –.

Most notably, the greatest job growth is anticipated for teachers, customer service representatives, and registered nurses over the next two quarters. – 3 –. Each of these categories is expected to grow by 5 percent through the remainder of the year. Moderate growth is expected for a majority of positions in the hospitality sector as the tourism industry continues to develop and vacation season begins. – 4 –.

To read the full report, which provides projections for more than twenty industries, visit: www.edwardsville.gov/trade_commission

164. What does the report discuss?
(A) Average local salaries.
(B) Workplace safety concerns.
(C) Future jobs in the area.
(D) Changes in consumer spending.

165. How often is the report published?
(A) Once a year.
(B) Twice a year.
(C) Every month.
(D) Every quarter.

166. The word "over" in paragraph 2, line 2, is closest in meaning to
(A) above.
(B) near.
(C) during.
(D) beyond.

167. In which of the positions marked [1], [2], [3] and [4] does the following sentence best belong?
"However, positions in manufacturing are expected to decline by 10 percent in the greater Edwardsville area."
(A) [1].
(B) [2].
(C) [3].
(D) [4].

Rankin Makes Large Donation to Save Old Springfield

March 30 — Springfield resident and architect Chester Rankin of Parchment Design Group announced yesterday that he is donating one million dollars over the next two years to the Save Old Springfield project. The contribution comes at a critical time, as the project's funding has been declining for the past three years. "We're thrilled to receive Mr. Rankin's generous gift." said Springfield Historical Society (SHS) president Maurice Bovine. "It will go a long way toward conserving the architectural cornerstones of our community."

Save Old Springfield was launched ten years ago by the Springfield Historical Society to restore and preserve buildings from the town's early years. It was originally funded through tax revenue. However, three years ago the town council decided to shift much of that funding away from the RHS and into a new land development initiative. Since then, financial support for the project has remained limited.

Five months ago, SHS began soliciting private donations from larger businesses in the region. "Along with a letter asking for support, we sent photographs of several historic buildings awaiting restoration." Mr. Bovine recalled. One such building was the house on Fordham Street where Chester Rankin grew up. "I didn't know about Mr. Rankin's personal connection to the property until he called me and asked how he could help," Mr. Bovine said. Springfield residents and community leaders have responded enthusiastically to news of the donation. The town council has also suggested putting honorary plaques in several historic landmarks to make the town more appealing to new residents, visitors, and businesses.

Mr. Rankin said in a statement, "When I was a child, I was inspired by the buildings in Springfield. They were instrumental in helping me choose my career. But this gift is not just about preserving the town's history. It's about investing in its future."

— Dieter Neubauer, Beat Reporter

168. When was the Save Old Springfield project started?
(A) Five months ago.
(B) Two years ago.
(C) Ten years ago.
(D) Three years ago.

169. According to the article, why did the project lose funding?
(A) Because the restoration work was completed.
(B) Because construction costs rose unexpectedly.
(C) Because Springfield's population had declined.
(D) Because the local government reduced its financial support.

170. What motivated Mr. Rankin to make the donation?
(A) A personal phone call from Mr. Bovine.
(B) The chance to design historic buildings.
(C) Pictures of his childhood home.
(D) Being chosen to develop new land in Springfield.

171. What does Mr. Rankin suggest about the buildings in Springfield?
(A) They are too expensive to maintain.
(B) They motivated him to become an architect.
(C) Local businesses should pay to restore them.
(D) Each one should have a plaque indicating the year it was built.

GO ON TO THE NEXT PAGE.

48-HOUR NOTICE OF INTENT TO ENTER APARTMENT

RESIDENT NAME(S): Davis, Marion
DATE: December 2
PROPERTY: 302 Walker Avenue
APT #: 18A

Dear Resident:

In order to serve you properly, it is necessary to enter your apartment from time to time to perform certain preventive maintenance procedures (such as changing HVAC filters), and to accompany and supervise certain contractors (such as pest control). While we try to make every effort possible to accommodate your schedule, there are times when we must enter your apartment in your absence to ensure continuity of our maintenance program and contracted services.

Your lease gives us the right, upon notification to you, to enter your apartment during normal business hours for the purposes of upkeep, to make repairs and to perform routine inspections. Your lease also provides that, in an emergency, we can enter your apartment without prior notice.

This letter shall serve as our notice to you that we will be entering your apartment on December 5, sometime between the hours of 9:00 a.m. and 5:00 p.m., to perform the following service:

____Pest Control   ____HVAC Filter Change   ____HVAC Coil Cleaning

__√__Other: **SMOKE DETECTOR MAINTENANCE**

Please make certain that the Management Office has keys to any apartment front door locks you may have installed since moving in. Your lease specifically states that you may not change your locks without the prior written permission of the management, and that you must provide management with a key to any new locks installed. If we are unable to gain entrance to your apartment because of the presence of unauthorized locks, we will be forced to begin eviction proceedings against you.

Please call me should you have any questions. Thank you very much.

Sincerely,

Fred Timmons, Property Manager

cc: Resident File

---

172. What is this notice mainly about?
(A) Apartment maintenance.
(B) Security guidelines.
(C) Guest policies.
(D) Management office hours.

173. What will happen on December 5th?
(A) The elevator won't be in service.
(B) Marion Davis will go out of town.
(C) Lobby keys will no longer work.
(D) The smoke detectors will be tested.

174. What might happen if access cannot be gained to Marion Davis's apartment?
(A) A fire could break out.
(B) The smoke detectors will go off.
(C) She could be evicted.
(D) A locksmith will be called.

175. What does the lease specifically prohibit without prior written permission?
(A) Spraying for bugs.
(B) Smoking indoors.
(C) Changing the locks.
(D) Painting the interior.

GO ON TO THE NEXT PAGE.

To: Greg Espinosa
From: Thad Sayer
Date: Tuesday, January 24
Subject: Phone issue

Dear Greg,

I'm writing to discuss an issue related to my recent move to room 7054. I've taken over Ash Gropius' old office and phone number, as she has taken an extended leave from work. Apparently, customers were not informed about this, and consequently, I have received, on average, over thirty calls a day from her customer accounts. It appears as though the employee directory has not yet been changed to let them know that: (A) She is not here; and (B) Mo-Chien Huang is handling her accounts in the meantime. To have to take so many calls that are not intended for me is so time-consuming and distracting. Would it be possible to change the extension number or connect my old extension number 5-7025 to room 7054? I would greatly appreciate your help.

Thank you very much.

Thad Sayer

STAFF DIRECTORY

Employee name	Ext. number
Garrett Sullivan	5-7079
Ash Gropius	5-7054
Mo-Chien Huang	4-6121
Deidre Kinski	5-7043
Thad Sayer	5-7025
J.T. Carpenter	4-6089
Benny Quayle	5-7065

A "4" prefix designates an office located on the fourth floor

A "5" prefix designates an office located on the fifth floor

176. According to the list, who works on the fourth floor?
(A) Garett Sullivan.
(B) Maria Kinski.
(C) J.T. Carpenter.
(D) Benny Quayle.

177. What is Thad Sayer's current extension number?
(A) 5-7025.
(B) 5-7054.
(C) 5-7065.
(D) 5-7079.

178. In the e-mail, the word "leave" in paragraph 1 in line 3 is closest in meaning to
(A) removal.
(B) absence.
(C) sequence.
(D) departure.

179. What does Thad Sayer say about Mo-Chien Huang?
(A) He has been assigned a certain number of clients.
(B) His employee directory information has not been updated.
(C) He is gathering information for the employee directory.
(D) His technical problems have been resolved.

180. What does Thad Sayer mention in his e-mail?
(A) He has not received a telephone directory.
(B) His office is on the second floor.
(C) He is being unnecessarily interrupted at work.
(D) His telephone isn't functioning properly.

GO ON TO THE NEXT PAGE.

Chris Rossini, Manager
Aldo's Market
374 Lexington Pkwy N
St. Paul, MN 55104

September 27

Dear Mr. Rossini,

Upon reviewing the receipt for my recent purchase at your store, I noticed that I was charged for an extra jar of mayonnaise. I'm certain that I purchased only one jar, but I didn't go back to your store, as I was leaving town for a long weekend the next day. In my haste to get home, I didn't realize the error that day. The cashier I recall was courteous but seemed unfamiliar with your equipment.

Since I am one of your longtime satisfied customers, I hope you will agree to correct this error. I would be happy to accept a credit for the same amount toward a future purchase. I have enclosed the receipt of purchase so that you can verify and process the credit, as appropriate. Please contact me at g_blankfeld@lemail if you have any further questions.

Sincerely
Gloria Blankfeld

```
ALDO'S MARKET
374 Lexington Pkwy N
St. Paul, MN 55104
Thursday, September 21 12:34:09
#AM-29384
Receipt

1 Deli Select Sandwich — PASTRAMI        $4.45
1 Deli Select Sandwich — TURKEY          $3.85
12 Blueberry muffins   @1.50             $15.00
1 16oz. Gold Star mayonnaise             $3.15
1 16oz. Gold Star mayonnaise             $3.15
1 Newspaper                              $1.50

SUBTOTAL                         $31.00
STATE SALES TAX (8.75%)          $2.72

TOTAL                            $33.72

Cashier    T. Shipp

Thank you for shopping at Aldo's
Open every day 9 AM - 9 PM
```

181. What most likely caused the problem?
(A) The cashier's inexperience.
(B) Ms. Blankfeld's hurry to leave the store.
(C) Faulty equipment at the store.
(D) An incorrectly marked price.

182. When did Ms. Blankfeld leave for a trip?
(A) On September 21.
(B) On September 22.
(C) On September 27.
(D) On September 28.

183. What is NOT on the receipt?
(A) The cashier's name.
(B) The manager's name.
(C) The date and time of the transaction.
(D) The store's hours.

184. What can be inferred about Ms. Blankfeld?
(A) She has received good service at the store before.
(B) She was late for work because of the incident.
(C) She is moving away from St. Paul.
(D) She is a good friend of Chris Rossini.

185. What is the purpose of Ms. Blankfeld's letter?
(A) To place an order for groceries to be delivered.
(B) To complain about a poorly-made sandwich.
(C) To suggest a product placement.
(D) To request a credit for an extra charge.

GO ON TO THE NEXT PAGE.

Books by Dick Rivers

The Evolution of Music

Where did it all begin? Rivers visually chronicles the evolution of music through the centuries, from traditional folk music to contemporary dance music.

Look Past the Glass

Rivers captures the creative process of some of the top musicians from Los Angeles to London. Spanning almost twenty years, the book is filled with Rivers's photographs and shows what goes on in recording studios before music is released to the masses.

And The Cradle Will Rock: My Story

An amusing memoir about growing up in the music and entertainment world. Rivers writes about his unconventional upbringing in Hollywood with parents who began as touring musicians before launching their own record label.

Revolving Doors: A Decade of Taste

A collection of Rivers's images collected throughout a decade of popular music and revealing what was popular, what was considered "uncool", and then what was popular once again after falling out of favor.

EVENING PROGRAMMING, OCTOBER 3

6:00 PM — In the Kitchen with Kim
Host Kim Pauley talks about the latest super foods; what they are, what they offer, and how best to prepare them. Featured recipes will be available on our website after tonight's show.

7:00 PM — Shooting from the Hip
Host Lucy Slate interviews photographer and author Dick Rivers about what prompted him to write his latest book about his childhood. He shares stories about what it was like to grow up in the entertainment industry.

8:00 PM — Digital Nation
Host Gary Flax focuses on the latest digital technology. He discusses products that are really innovative and useful and identifies those that are not.

Audio Archive   Talent   Sponsors

GO ON TO THE NEXT PAGE.

From:	clarisemay@onemail.com
To:	comments@citrus3radio.com
Re:	Dick Rivers/Shooting from the Hip
Date:	October 4

I discovered CITRUS3 Radio over 15 years ago and have been a regular listener of your evening programming for at least a decade. I just want to say how much I enjoy your newest program, Shooting from the Hip, hosted by Lucy Slate. I've been interested in many of the authors that have been featured on the show so far, but last evening's guest was especially entertaining. I remember Dick from when he was a little boy. I worked with his parents when they lived in Hollywood, and I recall seeing Dick in his parents' studio most days when most kids were in school. So I was thrilled to learn that he has written about his childhood, and I look forward to reading his new book. Thank you for the excellent programming.

Clarise May

186. What is one common feature in all of Mr. Rivers's books?
(A) They contain personal photographs.
(B) They focus on amateur musicians.
(C) They are set in Hollywood.
(D) They follow events over multiple years.

187. What book did Mr. Rivers discuss on CITRUS3 Radio?
(A) The Evolution of Music
(B) Look Past the Glass
(C) And the Cradle Will Rock: My Story
(D) Revolving Doors: A Decade of Taste

188. What is indicated about Shooting from the Hip?
(A) It is hosted by Kim Pauley.
(B) It was moved to a new time.
(C) It is broadcast every morning at 7:00.
(D) It was recently added to CITRUS3 Radio.

189. In the e-mail, the word "regular" in line 1 is closest in meaning to
(A) frequent.
(B) complete.
(C) curious.
(D) typical.

190. What is probably true about Ms. May?
(A) She was featured on Digital Nation.
(B) She hosts a radio program.
(C) She has worked in the music industry.
(D) She has interviewed Mr. Rivers.

https:/www.crenshawbush.com/roverelite

Crenshaw & Bush

ROVER ELITE LUGGAGE SET

Weekender Carry-On	**$149**
International Upright Spinner	**$349**
Large Expandable Spinner	**$549**

Complete set $949 (save 10%)

Colors: Elegant Slate (coming soon—Silver Ice)

Details:

Rover Elite is a coordinated collection that combines hard spinner cases with soft companion pieces. Take them together and get rolling or remove one and conveniently carry it with you.

Designed for hard use, Rover Elite is the world's only CX™ expandable hardside collection. The Rover Elite set features three pieces that are both lightweight and durable.

- Expandable central pockets
- Omni-directional wheels
- Easy-opening, tight-sealing clasps

GO ON TO THE NEXT PAGE.

CRENSHAW & BUSH
ROVER ELITE LUGGAGE SET

✪✪✪

Fiona V. Feltham

July 16

I frequently travel for business, often carrying perishable samples with me on the plane. Most carry-ons these days are soft-sided, so it was a relief to find something that offers adequate protection. I've been mostly happy with the carry-on, but the larger bags have caused some problems. My Elegant Slate spinners look so similar to everyone else's that other travelers have taken them by mistake on several occasions! More variety would be nice.

I also have some concerns about the mechanical elements of this set. In particular, the retraction mechanism of the handle is stiff and frequently gets stuck in the extended position.

July 17

Dear Ms. Feltham,

We're sorry to hear about your trouble with our product. As a result of feedback like yours, we've introduced a new color option. If you contact us at: support@crenshawbush.com, we'll send you, in our attractive new color, a duplicate of the large expandable spinner to complement your Rover Elite set. Note that this gift will be sent to you after you verify that you posted the July 16 review.

We also appreciate your feedback about our luggage components. Rest assured that our handle mechanism has been proven to withstand years' worth of rough treatment, retracting and extending smoothly over 10,000 times under stressful conditions in our laboratories.

Walter Goloub, Crenshaw & Bush customer service

191. What does Ms. Feltham write about her luggage?
(A) She likes the color.
(B) The cases are too large.
(C) She purchased the bags recently.
(D) The carry-on protects her samples.

192. In the review, the word "concerns" in paragraph 2, line 1, is closest in meaning to
(A) arrangements.
(B) reservations.
(C) experiences.
(D) features.

193. What does Mr. Goloub offer to Ms. Feltham?
(A) A full set of Silver Ice luggage.
(B) A full set of Elegant Slate luggage.
(C) A large Silver Ice suitcase.
(D) A small Elegant Slate carry-on.

194. What must Ms. Feltham do in order to receive a gift from Crenshaw & Bush?
(A) Retract negative feedback given on a website.
(B) Send a package containing a defective suitcase.
(C) Prove that she is the author of a product review.
(D) Complete a survey about new products.

195. What does Mr. Goloub indicate about the handles of the suitcases?
(A) They are as large as possible for the size of the suitcase.
(B) They are less reliable than those of previous models.
(C) They have been thoroughly tested.
(D) They have been redesigned to expand and retract more easily.

GO ON TO THE NEXT PAGE.

MARIE KONDO INTERIORS

7722 West Viceroy ⊙ St.Paul

DECEMBER 28-29
ANNUAL YEAR-END
CLEARANCE SALE

Phone: (502) 437-1100
Monday to Friday, 9 A.M. to 5 P.M.

Please note that the store will close at 3:00 P.M. on Thursday, December 27 in order to prepare for the sale.

Sales prices are available on both in-store and online purchases.

Sign up for Marie Kondo Interiors' VIP membership to become eligible for free delivery.

Our trained sales staff is available to answer any questions.

Floor coverings

10% off

———

Window furnishings

10% off

———

Bedroom & living room furniture

25% off

———

Kitchen & dining room furniture

25% off

———

Home décor items

40% off

To: All employees

From: Gail Gossamer

Subject: Schedule

Date: December 1

To all employees,

We are adding an overnight shift on December 27 and will need employees to record inventory, mark prices, and move goods and merchandise. I have arranged a special treat from Stump's so that all volunteers will have breakfast in addition to time-and-a-half pay during the shift. Please notify me by December 7 if you are available.

Sincerely,
Gail Gossamer
Store Manager

GO ON TO THE NEXT PAGE.

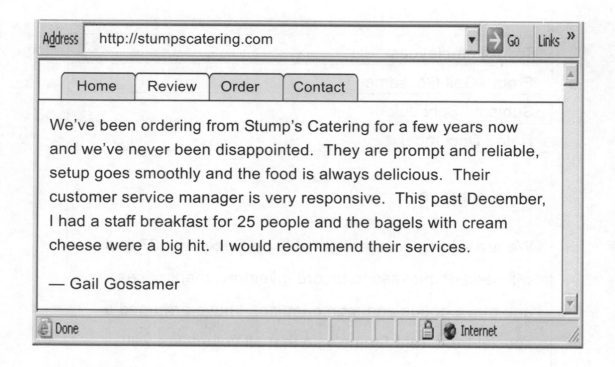

Address http://stumpscatering.com ▼ → Go Links »

| Home | Review | Order | Contact |

We've been ordering from Stump's Catering for a few years now and we've never been disappointed. They are prompt and reliable, setup goes smoothly and the food is always delicious. Their customer service manager is very responsive. This past December, I had a staff breakfast for 25 people and the bagels with cream cheese were a big hit. I would recommend their services.

— Gail Gossamer

Done 🔒 🌐 Internet

196. According to the advertisement, what will happen on December 27?
(A) Some new merchandise will arrive.
(B) A store will close early.
(C) A membership program will begin.
(D) A furniture sale will take place.

197. What does Ms. Gossamer ask employees to do?
(A) Prepare for an annual event.
(B) Pay attention to details.
(C) Attend some training sessions.
(D) Demonstrate an assembly process.

198. In the e-mail, the word "arranged" in paragraph 1, line 3 is closest in meaning to
(A) displayed.
(B) positioned.
(C) planned.
(D) adjusted.

199. How many employees responded to Ms. Gossamer's request?
(A) 10.
(B) 25.
(C) 40.
(D) 100.

200. What is NOT mentioned in the online review?
(A) The quality of food.
(B) The timeliness of delivery.
(C) The level of customer service.
(D) The competitiveness of the price.

Stop! This is the end of the test. If you finish before time is called, you may go back to Parts 5, 6, and 7 and check your work.

New TOEIC Listening Script

PART 1

1. (   ) (A) Some people are in a gymnasium.
    (B) Some people are in a bank.
    (C) Some people are in a supermarket.
    (D) Some people are in an airport.

2. (   ) (A) The man is preparing some food.
    (B) The man is washing some dishes.
    (C) The man is making some copies.
    (D) The man is tying his shoes.

3. (   ) (A) Some people are seated at an outdoor café.
    (B) Some people are sitting in a doctor's waiting room.
    (C) Some people are standing on a bridge.
    (D) Some people are running on a beach.

4. (   ) (A) The man is replacing a light bulb.
    (B) The man is operating some machinery in a warehouse.
    (C) The man is making a delivery to a private home.
    (D) The man is opening a bunch of packages.

5. (   ) (A) Some students are taking an exam in a large classroom.
    (B) Some students are watching a football game in a stadium.
    (C) Some students are graduating from college.
    (D) Some students are talking in the library.

6. (   ) (A) Some tourists are riding a boat.
    (B) Some tourists are looking at a map.
    (C) Some tourists are taking pictures.
    (D) Some tourists are waiting in line.

GO ON TO THE NEXT PAGE.

PART 2

7. (　　) Where is the trade expo being held this year?
   - (A) In Los Angeles.
   - (B) I've made a list of candidates.
   - (C) Try this one.

8. (　　) How often does the hotel shuttle bus go to the airport?
   - (A) Next to the fitness room.
   - (B) Every 20 minutes.
   - (C) It's pretty warm.

9. (　　) When is the new retail shop opening?
   - (A) That's what I heard.
   - (B) In late October.
   - (C) A dinner menu.

10. (　　) Do you know where the post office is?
    - (A) He can't attend today.
    - (B) At least that many.
    - (C) Yes, it's around the corner.

11. (　　) I found Ronald's company ID badge in the restroom.
    - (A) You can leave it on his desk.
    - (B) Would you mind doing it?
    - (C) In the company newsletter.

12. (　　) Did you find a DJ for the annual company party yet?
    - (A) I'm not in charge of the entertainment.
    - (B) Four or five tickets.
    - (C) She made a wise decision.

13. (　　) When are you going to submit the budget report?
    - (A) He's a photographer for the local paper.
    - (B) It'll be ready by the end of the day.
    - (C) That's more money than expected.

14. (　　) What's the minimum education requirement for the job?
    - (A) Yes, I wear contact lenses.
    - (B) I'm waiting for a response.
    - (C) A bachelor's degree in engineering.

15. (　　) Could you review this proposal?
　　　　(A) I may have time tomorrow.
　　　　(B) Make a reservation, please.
　　　　(C) Mike, Joe, and Anna.

16. (　　) What are the shipping options for mailing this package?
　　　　(A) Let's shut the window.
　　　　(B) In the conference room.
　　　　(C) Overnight or three-day delivery.

17. (　　) Would you care to try a sample of our new organic cookie?
　　　　(A) I never knew that.
　　　　(B) That's a good point.
　　　　(C) Are there peanuts in it?

18. (　　) Didn't you say Paulina Rogers would be on this flight?
　　　　(A) She's sitting in row 15.
　　　　(B) I'll look at the results again.
　　　　(C) A repair estimate.

19. (　　) Where can I find the printer ink cartridges?
　　　　(A) It's very fast.
　　　　(B) Aren't they in the storage closet?
　　　　(C) Usually every evening.

20. (　　) You've been to the World Trade Center before, right?
　　　　(A) Ms. Wilson has.
　　　　(B) These shoes are tight.
　　　　(C) I'm near-sighted.

21. (　　) Can I get you something else or would you like the bill?
　　　　(A) At the top of the hill.
　　　　(B) We loved it.
　　　　(C) I'll have another cup of coffee.

22. (　　) What did you think of Sandra Park's job interview?
　　　　(A) Yes, I met him last week.
　　　　(B) She seems highly qualified.
　　　　(C) At the job fair in Seattle.

GO ON TO THE NEXT PAGE.

23. (　　) Could I borrow your stapler for a minute?
    (A) The clock is on the wall.
    (B) Of course, here you go.
    (C) It was a great event.

24. (　　) How much does the position pay?
    (A) Mary is checking the inventory now.
    (B) I prefer to live by the train station.
    (C) $25 an hour.

25. (　　) I e-mailed you about the meeting, didn't I?
    (A) I haven't checked my mail yet.
    (B) Near the bank.
    (C) He really enjoyed the experience.

26. (　　) Do you know which floor the marketing office is on?
    (A) The lights turn on automatically.
    (B) The forecast is out for December.
    (C) They've moved, so I'm not sure.

27. (　　) I don't know how to download mobile phone applications.
    (A) The road is closed.
    (B) It isn't difficult.
    (C) A notarized copy of your birth certificate.

28. (　　) When is the annual company charity event?
    (A) It's held every March.
    (B) Here's the conference schedule.
    (C) About innovation.

29. (　　) Has the print shop received our shipment of paper?
    (A) That's a good idea.
    (B) Yes, they just confirmed it.
    (C) I prefer this painting.

30. (　　) Do you want Louis or Tiffany to be at the product launch tomorrow?
    (A) I thought you were going.
    (B) That lunch was delicious.
    (C) Sure, it was quite exciting.

31. (   ) Why are the clients coming so early?
      (A) In the next building.
      (B) You'll have to ask Mr. Pruitt.
      (C) Yes, please come in.

PART 3

Questions 32 through 34 *refer to the following conversation.*

W : Thomas, what's the status on the grant proposal for tomorrow? Is your video presentation ready to go?

M : I'm in the final stretch, Maryanne. Just… a… couple of…

W : You realize this presentation will make or break us. I get nervous when things come down to the last minute. If we blow this, our wildlife preservation project is dead.

M : Of course. To be honest, the only thing I'm missing is the interview with the African hunter. You said you had a copy of the clip, but you never sent it to me.

W : I thought I e-mailed it to you already. I'll re-send it as soon as I get back to my desk.

M : Thanks. It'll probably be a good idea to double-check the laptop in the conference room. So after lunch, I'll make sure that the computer is properly connected to display videos.

32. (   ) What are the speakers discussing?
      (A) A presentation.
      (B) A television show.
      (C) A website.
      (D) A bank loan.

33. (   ) What does the man say he is missing?
      (A) A signature.
      (B) A video clip.
      (C) A password.
      (D) An e-mail address.

34. (   ) What does the man say he will do after lunch?
      (A) Contact a journalist.
      (B) Review some data.
      (C) Check a computer.
      (D) Write a proposal.

GO ON TO THE NEXT PAGE.

W : Hi, I recently came across a flyer for a community clean-up event next month. It said I should sign up to be a neighborhood captain here at City Hall. Who do I need to talk to about this?

M : Um, there's been a change in plans. Originally, the registration office was here, but it has been moved to the courthouse. We had new flyers made, but apparently a lot of the old fliers are still posted.

W : I see. Well, that's actually quite convenient for me. My office is across the street from the courthouse, so I can stop by this afternoon. By the way, if you have any extra flyers with the correct information, I could pass them around to my friends at work.

35. (   ) Why did the woman stop by City Hall?
   (A) To claim a lost item.
   (B) To speak with an administrator.
   (C) To register for an event.
   (D) To file for a permit.

36. (   ) Where is the woman instructed to go?
   (A) To a local park.
   (B) To the courthouse.
   (C) To a department store.
   (D) To a community center.

37. (   ) What does the woman ask for?
   (A) Some updated flyers.
   (B) A building directory.
   (C) A map of the city.
   (D) A list of cleaning companies.

W : Hi, I'm calling about my credit card bill. I paid it online two weeks ago, but today I received a notice saying I was being charged a late fee of $25. That can't be right. I submitted the payment three days before the due date.

M : First, thanks for calling Tripp Financial and being a loyal customer. I can reverse that charge. You see, there was a problem with our online bill payment system, and late fees were mistakenly charged to thousands of customers.

W : Well, I want to make sure that my interest rate hasn't been automatically raised because of the late fee. Can you confirm that for me?

M : I understand. If you just give me your account number, I'll pull up your information.

38. (   ) Why is the woman calling?
   (A) To answer a question.
   (B) To report an incorrect charge.
   (C) To close an account.
   (D) To ask about a policy.

39. (   ) What is the woman also concerned about?
   (A) Frequent flyer miles.
   (B) Membership fees.
   (C) Interest rates.
   (D) Identity theft.

40. (   ) What does the man ask for?
   (A) A payment date.
   (B) A street address.
   (C) An account number.
   (D) A password.

Questions 41 through 43 _refer to the following conversation between three speakers._

M : Hi, ladies. I've come up with a new concept for the website, and I think it will drive more traffic and boost our sales. Do you have time today to sit down and give me some feedback?

Woman UK : Unfortunately, this afternoon I've got a budget review meeting. But I'm free most of tomorrow.

Woman US : I'm booked solid today as well. If you want to meet tomorrow, I'm available from 10:00 a.m. until lunch. After that, I've got interviews for the open IT position.

M : OK, how about we meet tomorrow at 10 in my office? That will give me some time to tweak a couple of elements and bring the whole concept into focus.

41. (   ) What is the conversation mainly about?
   (A) A website.
   (B) A sales report.
   (C) A budget review.
   (D) A job interview.

42. (   ) What does the man want to do?
   (A) Implement a new hiring policy.
   (B) Begin a renovation project.
   (C) Implement an advertising campaign.
   (D) Discuss an idea.

GO ON TO THE NEXT PAGE.

43. (　　) What does the man say he will do before the meeting?
    (A) Read a resume.
    (B) Hire a programmer.
    (C) Print some flyers.
    (D) Revise a concept.

Questions 44 through 46 refer to the following conversation.

M : Hey, Lisa. Congrats on closing the Shelby deal. Great job! Listen, I have a favor to ask. The Tokyo client wants to catch an earlier flight to New York for the weekend, so I need to meet with him this afternoon. So… I was hoping you wouldn't mind leading the intern training session at 3:30. I'll make it up to you, I promise.

W : I would be happy to, Jeff, but I'm having lunch with Dave Shelby to celebrate the deal. It's way out at his country club in Oak Brook, so I'm taking the rest of the afternoon off. Why don't you ask Tim?

M : I thought he was on vacation this week.

W : No, he was working from home Monday through Thursday. He'll be here today at 10:30. And I'm pretty sure his schedule is clear this afternoon.

44. (　　) What does the man want the woman to do?
    (A) Have lunch with a client.
    (B) Lead a training session.
    (C) Stay late.
    (D) Work from home.

45. (　　) What does the woman suggest?
    (A) Switching offices.
    (B) Taking a later flight.
    (C) Canceling a meeting.
    (D) Asking a co-worker.

46. (　　) When is the conversation most likely taking place?
    (A) On Monday.
    (B) On Thursday.
    (C) On Friday.
    (D) On Saturday.

Questions 47 through 49 refer to the following conversation.

M : Hi, this is Bob Reese. I have a storage space at your facility, and I'm calling because I lost the key to the lock. I really need to get some sporting equipment out of there for a softball tournament tomorrow.

W : That's not a problem, Bob. Come by the rental office and I'll loan you a copy of our key. We're open until 9:00 p.m. tonight.

M : What a relief! I'm on my way now. Oh, can I make a copy of the loaner key? It might take a few days…

W : We can talk about that when you get here, Bob. See you then.

47. (   ) Why is the man calling?
       (A) To obtain a document.
       (B) To ask about a moving service.
       (C) To check on an order.
       (D) To report a lost key.

48. (   ) What does the woman suggest that the man do?
       (A) Send her an e-mail.
       (B) Come to her office.
       (C) Bring a copy of an invoice.
       (D) Speak with the maintenance department.

49. (   ) What does the man ask about?
       (A) Changing a schedule.
       (B) Finding an office location.
       (C) Selecting a moving date.
       (D) Making a duplicate key.

Questions 50 through 52 *refer to the following conversation.*

W : Hi, Simon. You know, everybody is thrilled that you transferred to the corporate sales division. I understand you've already opened a few major accounts. So… what do you think about the position so far?

M : I'm travelling a lot more than I thought I would, but overall, I'm very happy. This month, I've already met with a dozen engineering firms interested in subscribing to our network services.

W : Well, we have two new sales associates starting next week. So, you shouldn't have to travel so much in the future. You'll be able to concentrate on managing your accounts as opposed to landing them.

50. (   ) What area does the man work in?
       (A) Personnel.
       (B) Engineering.
       (C) Sales.
       (D) Advertising.

GO ON TO THE NEXT PAGE.

51. (   ) What surprised the man about his new position?
    (A) The amount of paperwork.
    (B) The speed of the network.
    (C) The frequency of travel.
    (D) The long hours.

52. (   ) What has the company done recently?
    (A) Upgraded a system.
    (B) Discontinued a product.
    (C) Launched a marketing campaign.
    (D) Hired new employees.

Questions 53 through 55 *refer to the following conversation.*

M : Yes, good afternoon. May I please speak with Donna Carlson? This is Rich Tilley from the consumer credit division at Mega National Bank.

W : Hi, Rich. This is Donna. What can I do for you?

M : Ms. Carlson, I'm calling in reference to some suspicious activity on your credit card account. The system detected an unusually large transaction. But first, for your protection, may I have the last four digits of your Social Security number?

W : Sure, 5-5-0-2. Is this about the dining room set I just bought at Wilson's Furniture?

M : Um, yes. Did you make a purchase of $3,294.77 on October 5?

53. (   ) Where does the man work?
    (A) At a bank.
    (B) At a furniture store.
    (C) At a post office.
    (D) At a news organization.

54. (   ) Why is the man contacting the woman?
    (A) A new credit card will be issued.
    (B) A transaction has been reversed.
    (C) A delivery was sent to a wrong address.
    (D) A large amount was charged to her account.

55. (   ) What did the woman most likely do?
    (A) Make a complaint.
    (B) Buy some furniture.
    (C) Lose her mobile phone.
    (D) Take out a loan.

W : You've been to that fancy Chinese restaurant on Field Street, haven't you? They have facilities for large events, right? I'm in charge of the investor's banquet next month and I need to find a place that could accommodate a group of 50.

M : Yeah, you mean Din Yang Sun. My cousin had his wedding reception in the Mandarin Room—it's huge, seats 200 people. But I think they have rooms for smaller functions, too.

W : How's the food?

M : Great Cantonese-style cuisine. I took some clients from Hong Kong to lunch there a few days ago and they loved it! One guy said it was as good as the food from his hometown. Very authentic. It's pricey, though. Lunch for five was $400 plus service charge.

W : That's good to know, but money really isn't an object for this event.

56. (   ) What event are the speakers discussing?
    (A) A banquet.
    (B) A wedding.
    (C) A business trip.
    (D) A client.

57. (   ) What does the man say about the restaurant?
    (A) Service is slow.
    (B) The menu needs revision.
    (C) The food is very good.
    (D) Seating is limited.

58. (   ) What does the woman imply?
    (A) She doesn't have enough time to finish her work.
    (B) Many employees can't attend the event.
    (C) The banquet is not important.
    (D) Her budget is unlimited.

Woman US : Satoshi, Louisa from the Gardening Center is here to look at our outdoor seating area.

M : Hi, Louisa. The patio's here on the north side of the café, so it doesn't get much direct sunlight. But I'd like to have as many plants as possible to create a comfortable space for our customers to enjoy their coffee.

GO ON TO THE NEXT PAGE.

Woman UK : Well, there are quite a few species of potted plants that will thrive in that space with indirect sunlight. You should come by the Garden Center tomorrow to see them.

M : Would you mind e-mailing me some photos instead? Some tables are being delivered tomorrow, so I'll need to stay here all day.

59. (　　) Where is the conversation taking place?
      (A) At a park.
      (B) At a café.
      (C) At a furniture store.
      (D) At a supermarket.

60. (　　) What does Louisa suggest that the man do?
      (A) Open a window.
      (B) Use a coupon.
      (C) Visit a plant shop.
      (D) Extend business hours.

61. (　　) What does the man ask Louisa for?
      (A) A list of prices.
      (B) A deadline extension.
      (C) Some coffee.
      (D) Some photographs.

Questions 62 through 64 *refer to the following conversation and list.*

M : Hey, Maureen. I'm so excited that GriffCo is sponsoring the 10k run for charity again this year. It's a major event with hundreds of participants, so it should be great exposure for us.

W : Oh, that reminds me. Have you looked over this list of graphic design firms we're considering to produce the T-shirts? We need them at least a week in advance of the event, so we have to make a decision soon.

M : Let me see what you've got there. Hmm. Avatar Studios does some amazing stuff, but our budget has been cut in half from last year's race.

W : You're right. How about these guys in Cleveland? They offer quick turnaround times and their prices are affordable.

62. (　　) What is the company sponsoring?
      (A) A pancake breakfast.
      (B) A charity run.
      (C) A golf outing.
      (D) A weekend retreat.

63. (　　) What is the man concerned about?
  - (A) A limited budget.
  - (B) A weather forecast.
  - (C) A safety issue.
  - (D) An ad campaign.

64. (　　) Look at the graphic. Which company do the speakers choose?
  - (A) Avatar Studios
  - (B) Buckeye Silk Screen Co.
  - (C) Icon Design
  - (D) Taylor & Martin

Company	Location
Avatar Studios	Columbus
Taylor & Martin	Columbus
Buckeye Silk Screen Co.	Cleveland
Icon Graphic	Cincinnati

Questions 65 through 67 refer to the following conversation and building directory.

W : I just parked in the underground garage and I'm wondering if it's free for visitors on official business. I received this ticket from the automated machine when I entered, but...

M : Actually, if you have an appointment with one of our resident medical professionals, I can validate your ticket so you don't have to pay upon exiting.

W : That's what I wanted to hear. I have a 4:30 appointment to see Dr. Gupta, but I don't see his name on the building directory. Am I even in the right place?

M : Dr. Gupta is the newest addition to the building and just moved in last Friday. So we haven't had time to change the directory. You'll find him in Suite 110.

65. (　　) What is the purpose of the woman's visit?
  - (A) To have her car serviced.
  - (B) To deliver a package.
  - (C) To see a doctor.
  - (D) To attend a seminar.

GO ON TO THE NEXT PAGE.

66. (　　) What can the man do for the woman?
    (A) Validate her parking.
    (B) Reschedule her appointment.
    (C) Park her car.
    (D) Issue a rain check.

67. (　　) Look at the graphic. Which office name has to be updated on the building directory?
    (A) Unger Fertility Clinic
    (B) Kreutz Eye Care
    (C) Dr. Karl Edwards, OB-GYN
    (D) Smithson Cosmetic Surgery

DIRECTORY	
Unger Fertility Clinic	Suite 101
Dr. Karl Edwards, OB-GYN	Suite 110
Smithson Cosmetic Surgery	Suite 201
Kreutz Eye Care	Suite 210
Weiner & Associates	Suite 301

Questions 68 through 70 _refer to the following conversation and map._

M : Joe's Pizza House, what would you like to order?

W : Hi, Joe. It's Vanessa. I'm on Mill Street by the bus stop right now. I've almost finished delivering the food orders, but this last one doesn't have an address on it.

M : Hmm, no address. Is there a name?

W : Uh, it's Dan Smith.

M : OK, let me look that up. The Smith order needs to be delivered to the Hazelton Apartment Building, Apartment 12.

W : Oh, yes, on Durham Road, directly across from the park. Thanks.

68. (　　) Who most likely is the woman?
   (A) A postal worker.
   (B) A delivery driver.
   (C) A repair technician.
   (D) A building manager.

69. (　　) What problem does the woman mention?
   (A) A package has been damaged.
   (B) A vehicle is not working.
   (C) Some residents are not home.
   (D) Some information is missing.

70. (　　) Look at the graphic. Where will the woman go next?
   (A) To building 1.
   (B) To building 2.
   (C) To building 3.
   (D) To building 4.

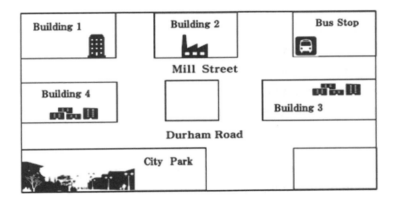

GO ON TO THE NEXT PAGE.

PART 4

Questions 71 through 73 *refer to the following telephone message.*

Hi Nina, it's Jeff. We should get started on the hiring process for our new restaurant. //Can you believe the grand opening is less than a month away?// We have a lot of resumes to read through. Are you available to meet tomorrow? If so, I'll e-mail the resumes I've received so far. And then, when we meet, we can compare which candidates we'd like to interview. Let me know if tomorrow works for you. Thanks.

71. (   ) What is the purpose of the message?
    (A) To arrange a meeting.
    (B) To confirm an order.
    (C) To apply for a job.
    (D) To make a reservation.

72. (   ) What does the speaker imply when he says, //"Can you believe the grand opening is less than a month away?"//?
    (A) Projects will be completed on time.
    (B) Decisions must be made quickly.
    (C) Appointments must be rescheduled.
    (D) Reservations will be hard to get.

73. (   ) What will the speaker most likely do after Nina replies?
    (A) E-mail some documents.
    (B) Make some phone calls.
    (C) Fill out an application.
    (D) Hire a manager.

Questions 74 through 76 *refer to the following talk.*

I'll now bring this meeting to order. As you know, we've been working to create a wildlife refuge on the outskirts of town, but unfortunately, we're still lacking the necessary funding to proceed. Now, we've received an offer from a local company to erect some fencing along Sunday Creek, but we're still far short of money to construct a bird habitat. I think we should contact some businesses in the community to see if they'd be willing to make a donation. So what I'd like us to do now is draw up a list of business owners who might be interested in helping with this project.

74. (   ) What is the talk mainly about?
     (A) Planning an annual celebration.
     (B) Analyzing traffic patterns.
     (C) Attracting visitors to a park.
     (D) Building a wildlife refuge.

75. (   ) What problem does the speaker mention?
     (A) Scheduling conflicts.
     (B) Insufficient funding.
     (C) Zoning laws.
     (D) Broken equipment.

76. (   ) What are listeners asked to do?
     (A) Make a list of business owners.
     (B) Volunteer for a project.
     (C) Donate some money.
     (D) Choose a location.

Questions 77 through 79 *refer to the following advertisement.*

Are you in the market for a new electronic device? Do you wonder what to do with your old computers, mobile phones, or other electronic devices you don't use anymore? Well, bring them in to Digital Depot! We'll take the hassle out of recycling your electronic devices and put money in your pocket. When you bring your old devices to Digital Depot, you'll receive a voucher for 25 percent off any non-sale item in stock. To find the Digital Depot location nearest you, visit our website at www.digitaldepot.com.

77. (   ) What service is being advertised?
     (A) Computer consulting.
     (B) Overnight delivery.
     (C) A training course.
     (D) A recycling program.

78. (   ) How can listeners receive a discount?
     (A) By completing a survey.
     (B) By visiting the website.
     (C) By recycling an electronic device.
     (D) By entering a lottery.

GO ON TO THE NEXT PAGE.

79. (   ) What does the speaker say can be found on a website?
      (A) Recycling information.
      (B) Discount vouchers.
      (C) Instructional videos.
      (D) Store locations.

Questions 80 through 82 *refer to the following announcement.*

Attention passengers traveling on Triad Air Flight 7G434 to San Antonio. Due to mechanical issues, the flight has been canceled. We apologize for the inconvenience, and request that all passengers proceed to the Triad Air customer service desk in the main concourse. An airline representative will book you on a different flight and onward to your final destination. While you're waiting, Triad Air representatives will provide you with complimentary snacks and drinks. Again, we regret the inconvenience and thank you for flying with Triad Air.

80. (   ) Where is the announcement being made?
      (A) At a shopping mall.
      (B) At an airport.
      (C) At a bus terminal.
      (D) At a train station.

81. (   ) What does the speaker ask listeners to do?
      (A) Return at a later time.
      (B) Go to the customer service desk.
      (C) Apply for a refund.
      (D) Contact another airline.

82. (   ) According to the speaker, what will be distributed?
      (A) Headphones.
      (B) Reading materials.
      (C) Hotel vouchers.
      (D) Refreshments.

Questions 83 through 85 *refer to the following talk.*

Guys, if you don't mind, I'd like to get started. Today, we'll be reviewing the latest customer survey results for our new bread maker, the Noxa 350. As you're all aware, the bread maker includes a lot of great new features. And our customers appreciate the upgrades. According to the survey, the most popular feature of the bread maker is the diamond-coated pan and kneading blade, which are scratchproof and easier to clean than our last model. But because of all the added features, //the user's manual is currently about 10 pages too long//. So, the editors will be working on that this week.

83. (   ) What is the main topic of the meeting?
    (A) A competitor's products.
    (B) An instructional video.
    (C) Survey results.
    (D) An online review.

84. (   ) What feature of the product does the speaker mention?
    (A) Remote control.
    (B) Color options.
    (C) Durability.
    (D) Easier cleaning.

85. (   ) What does the speaker imply when he says, //"the user's manual is currently about 10 pages too long"//?
    (A) Pages will be added to the manual.
    (B) The manual will be shortened.
    (C) The manual is available to download online.
    (D) Customers should read the manual thoroughly.

Questions 86 through 88 _refer to the following announcement._

Welcome, folks. We're happy to see all of you here at People Power Staffing agency today. As you may know, People Power specializes in the placement of employees in temporary and long-term positions across a wide range of industries from advertising to transportation. As time allows, you'll meet individually with our recruiting specialists who have the experience to match your skills with the needs of our client companies. Obviously, we have standing-room only here in this waiting room, so please be patient and the next available specialist will be with you. Now, to help speed up the process, I'd like everybody to make a copy of your photo ID. The copy machine is right over here.

GO ON TO THE NEXT PAGE.

86. (   ) What type of business does the speaker work for?
    (A) An employment agency.
    (B) A fitness center.
    (C) An advertising firm.
    (D) A shipping company.

87. (   ) What does the speaker imply by, //"standing-room only"//?
    (A) He is pointing out that the office will close soon.
    (B) He recommends that a project date be extended.
    (C) Some seats are still available.
    (D) The room is very crowded.

88. (   ) What does the speaker ask the listeners to do?
    (A) Make a copy of their identification.
    (B) Complete some paperwork.
    (C) Stand at attention.
    (D) Confirm their contact information.

Questions 89 through 91 _refer to the following talk._

Great to see everybody this morning. I hope your internship in our brokerage firm has been a good experience for you so far. Today, I want you to help us promote the upcoming investment seminar. The program will include a talk by hedge fund manager Mark Greenfield. So, I'd like each of you to take at least 100 flyers with you today and distribute them around the building. In addition to handing them out to brokers, you'll be visiting some of the local businesses in the area. Don't worry. I'll give you a map where I circled the places I want you to go. Please be back at the office no later then 3:00 p.m. Have a great day!

89. (   ) Where do the listeners work?
    (A) At a brokerage firm.
    (B) At an art gallery.
    (C) At a medical clinic.
    (D) At a hair salon.

90. (   ) What will the listeners be doing today?
    (A) Making trades.
    (B) Attending a seminar.
    (C) Distributing flyers.
    (D) Watching a film.

91. (   ) What has the speaker done for the listeners?
      (A) Decorated an office.
      (B) Marked locations on a map.
      (C) Written recommendation letters.
      (D) Provided theater tickets.

Questions 92 through 94 *refer to the following excerpt from a meeting.*

As director of this firm, it gives me tremendous pleasure to formally announce our nomination for this year's Excellence in Design Award. This is a testament to the hard work of everybody in this room. But I specifically want to point out the innovative design by Greg Stiles and his team for the Trenton Tower project. The design was so original that we've received inquiries from competing architectural firms. I'd like to ask Mr. Stiles to talk about what inspired his team to create this remarkable project.

92. (   ) What kind of business does the speaker work for?
      (A) A local jeweler.
      (B) A public relations agency.
      (C) A department store.
      (D) An architectural firm.

93. (   ) What is the speaker announcing?
      (A) A new partnership.
      (B) A groundbreaking ceremony.
      (C) An employee promotion.
      (D) An award nomination.

94. (   ) What does the speaker say about Greg Stiles's project?
      (A) It promoted collaboration across departments.
      (B) It led to changes to a company policy.
      (C) It attracted interest from competing firms.
      (D) It made use of eco-friendly materials.

Questions 95 through 97 *refer to the following recorded message and order form.*

Hi, this is Rachel Gretz from Village Supply. I'm calling for Hank Brady. Hank, I've just had a look at your most recent order and I wanted to follow up on the number of Post-It notes you've ordered. It seemed unusual that you'd want ten times the normal amount,

GO ON TO THE NEXT PAGE.

so I went ahead and adjusted the number to match your regular order. Call me back if the number was intentional. By the way, I'll be out of the office next week, so Terry Finch will be handling my accounts while I'm gone. Give him a call at 877-0909 extension 34 if you have any issues.

95. (   ) Look at the graphic. Which quantity on the order form will be changed?
    (A) 2.
    (B) 4.
    (C) 10.
    (D) 200.

ORDER FORM	
Item	**Quantity**
Inkjet cartridges (B&W)	10
Time cards (50 ct.)	2
Post-It notes (100 ct.)	200
Coffee filters (10 ct.)	4

96. (   ) What did the speaker say she did?
    (A) Adjusted the quantity of an order.
    (B) Gave a product demonstration.
    (C) Inspected a facility.
    (D) Went on vacation.

97. (   ) What does the speaker say about Terry Finch?
    (A) He will be training a new employee.
    (B) He will be taking care of some accounts.
    (C) He will deliver the shipment.
    (D) He will maintain the website.

Questions 98 through 100 _refer to an excerpt from a meeting and neighborhood map._

OK, guys, if I could have your attention, please. Business has been great at every one of our restaurant locations in Moreland Valley. And we've received a lot of inquiries about food delivery. Since we've never offered delivery before, I'd like to try it at just one location first. Although our Lakeview restaurant is the most central, I think it's best we start in the smallest neighborhood because that's the most residential location.

Plus, we've gotten a lot of requests from that area. We need to get the word out though, so let's take some time now to discuss how we can advertise this new service.

98. (   ) What type of business does the speaker own?
    (A) A chain of restaurants.
    (B) A flower shop.
    (C) A taxi service.
    (D) A local grocery store.

99. (   ) Look at the graphic. In which neighborhood does the speaker want to offer a new service?
    (A) North Park.
    (B) Lakeview.
    (C) Arlington Heights.
    (D) South Valley.

NEIGHBORHOOD MAP

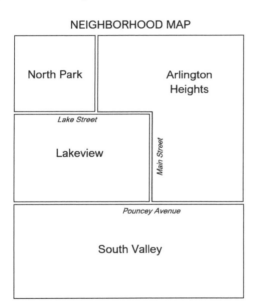

100. (   ) What does the speaker want to discuss next?
    (A) An updated vacation policy.
    (B) A renovation project.
    (C) Advertising strategies.
    (D) Hiring procedures.

GO ON TO THE NEXT PAGE.

NO TEST MATERIAL ON THIS PAGE

New TOEIC Speaking Test

Question 1: Read a Text Aloud

 **Question 1**

Directions: In this part of the test, you will read aloud the text on the screen. You will have 45 seconds to prepare. Then you will have 45 seconds to read the text aloud.

There's something disappointing about waking up earlier than necessary. It may be nice to doze in and out of sleep in the early morning hours, but it's especially upsetting if you cannot fall back asleep. There are specific conditions, including a fair number of sleep and mood disorders, which might cause early morning disturbances.

PREPARATION TIME
00 : 00 : 45

RESPONSE TIME
00 : 00 : 45

GO ON TO THE NEXT PAGE.

Question 2: Read a Text Aloud

 **Question 2**

Directions: In this part of the test, you will read aloud the text on the screen. You will have 45 seconds to prepare. Then you will have 45 seconds to read the text aloud.

The period immediately following Valentine's Day is a popular time for married couples to call it quits. One recent study suggested divorce filings rose by as much as 40 percent right after the holiday. Over the past two years we've seen an average increase of 40 percent in the number of requests for divorce lawyers around Valentine's Day, compared to the previous six months.

PREPARATION TIME
00 : 00 : 45

RESPONSE TIME
00 : 00 : 45

Question 3: Describe a Picture

 **Question 3**

Directions: In this part of the test, you will describe the picture on your screen in as much detail as you can. You will have 30 seconds to prepare your response. Then you will have 45 seconds to speak about the picture.

PREPARATION TIME
00 : 00 : 30

RESPONSE TIME
00 : 00 : 45

GO ON TO THE NEXT PAGE.

Question 3: Describe a Picture

答題範例

 **Question 3**

This may be a child's birthday party.

A boy is riding a pony.

He's wearing a hat.

There is a woman next to him.

She appears to be leading the pony.

She is wearing shorts and a shirt.

I don't see any other kids around.

The party is probably for the kid on the pony.

He doesn't look too enthusiastic about the situation.

They've dressed up the pony.

It's wearing a party hat and something on its neck.

I feel bad for the pony.

It's probably summer.

It's during the day.

It looks like a nice time for a party.

To be honest, I don't understand the attraction of ponies at
   birthday parties.

Every party with a pony I've ever been to ended badly.

Kids always wind up crying because one kid, usually the birthday
   boy or girl, won't get off the pony and give others a turn.

Questions 4-6: Respond to Questions

 **Question 4**

Directions: In this part of the test, you will answer three questions. For each question, begin responding immediately after you hear a beep. No preparation time is provided. You will have 15 seconds to respond to Questions 4 and 5 and 30 seconds to respond to Question 6.

Imagine that a pollster has asked you to participate in a survey about sports. You have agreed to answer some questions in a telephone interview.

Question 4

Do you play any sports?

RESPONSE TIME
00 : 00 : 15

Question 5

How much sports do you watch on TV?

RESPONSE TIME
00 : 00 : 15

Question 6

What do you like or dislike about sports?

RESPONSE TIME
00 : 00 : 30

GO ON TO THE NEXT PAGE.

Questions 4-6: Respond to Questions

答題範例

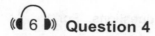 **Question 4**

Do you play any sports?

Answer

> I play some sports.
>
> I enjoy baseball and basketball.
>
> I also enjoy swimming.

 **Question 5**

How much sports do you watch on TV?

Answer

> Not that much.
>
> I might watch a ball game every so often.
>
> I also watch the Olympics.

Questions 4-6: Respond to Questions

 **Question 6**

What do you like or dislike about sports?

Answer

Well, I think they are basically good.

I like playing sports rather than watching.

I enjoy the exercise.

That's the point of sports, isn't it?

The physical exertion.

The competition.

What I dislike about sports is how commercial they've

become.

Athletes are ridiculously overpaid.

But so is everyone on TV, so that's why I never watch it.

GO ON TO THE NEXT PAGE.

Questions 7-9: Respond to Questions Using Information Provided

 **Question 7**

Directions: In this part of the test, you will answer three questions based on the information provided. You will have 30 seconds to read the information before the questions begin. For each question, begin responding immediately after you hear a beep. No additional preparation time is provided. You will have 15 seconds to respond to Questions 7 and 8 and 30 seconds to respond to Question 9.

SaltCON Board Game Convention

February 15-17

Do you like to play board games with your family and friends? Well, if you do, then come to the SaltCON Board Game Convention February 15-17 at the Sheraton Hotel in downtown Salt Lake City. Learn new games (like Ticket to Ride, Dominion, and Word on the Street), make new friends, play in tournaments—in short, have FUN!

Register now at www.saltcon.com for reduced rates—you can attend one, two, or all three days. Individual and group (family) rates available. Come join us at SaltCON: "Bringing the flavor back to gaming." Call the SaltCON hotline for more details (800)456-7890

Hi, I'm interested in the convention. Would you mind if I asked a few questions?

PREPARATION TIME
00 : 00 : 30

Question 7	Question 8	Question 9
RESPONSE TIME	RESPONSE TIME	RESPONSE TIME
00 : 00 : 15	00 : 00 : 15	00 : 00 : 30

Questions 7-9: Respond to Questions Using Information Provided

答題範例

 **Question 7**

When does the event take place?

Answer

> The conference begins on February 15.
>
> It's a three-day event.
>
> It ends on February 17.

 **Question 8**

What kind of activities will take place?

Answer

> Well, you can learn new games.
>
> You can compete in tournaments.
>
> You can make new friends who share your interest in
>
>   board games.

GO ON TO THE NEXT PAGE.

Questions 7-9: Respond to Questions Using Information Provided

 **Question 9**

How can I register for the event?

Answer

> You can register for reduced rates on our website.
>
> It's Saltcon.com.
>
> You can attend one, two, or three days.
>
> We offer special individual group rates.
>
> Depending upon your preferences, you can save a lot
>
>   of cash by registering on the website.
>
> Otherwise, you can just show up and pay at the door.
>
> If you're definitely planning to attend, I'd visit the
>
>   website.
>
> You still have plenty of time to register.
>
> We hope to see you there!

Question 10: Propose a Solution

 **Question 10**

Directions: In this part of the test, you will be presented with a problem and asked to propose a solution. You will have 30 seconds to prepare. Then you will have 60 seconds to speak. In your response, be sure to show that you recognize the problem, and propose a way of dealing with the problem.

In your response, be sure to

- show that you recognize the caller's problem, and
- propose a way of dealing with the problem.

PREPARATION TIME
00 : 00 : 30

RESPONSE TIME
00 : 01 : 00

GO ON TO THE NEXT PAGE

Question 10: Propose a Solution

答題範例

 **Question 10**

Voice Message

> Hello, this call is for Phillip's Towing Service. Yes, this is Bill Greer—you guys have helped me out before—anyway, I've been involved in an accident on Hauser Road, out near Terrace Park, and my car is damaged pretty bad. I ran off the road and into a tree, but you'll see that when you get here. Nobody's hurt but the car is not going anywhere. Aside from the fact that it's raining, the car is smoking and I smell gasoline. I'm wondering if I should get out of the car. I don't see any flames but the smoke is pretty thick. Anyway, please get back to me ASAP. My number is 654-1234.

Question 10: Propose a Solution

答題範例

Hello, Mr Greer.

This is Phil from Philip's Towing.

I'm sorry I missed your call.

Sounds like you've got yourself a problem there.

Of course, I remember you.

You drive that green BMW, right?

Anyway, I'm calling you back.

Tell me exactly where you're at and I can send one of my boys
over right away.

Your description is a bit vague, but that's OK.

Don't worry, we'll take care of the problem.

Now, if you hear this message, I need you to do me a favor.

Get out of the car.

First of all, I have no idea how bad the damage is.

There's hitting a tree and then there's smashing into a tree.

The one thing I know: smoke and gasoline are not a good match.

So again, get out of the car and as far away from it as possible.

Then call me back as soon as you can.

Talk to you soon.

GO ON TO THE NEXT PAGE.

Question 11: Express an Opinion

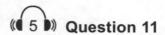 **Question 11**

Directions: In this part of the test, you will give your opinion about a specific topic. Be sure to say as much as you can in the time allowed. You will have 15 seconds to prepare. Then you will have 60 seconds to speak.

The increasingly rapid pace of life today causes more problems than it solves. Do you agree or disagree with this statement? Give reasons and examples to support your opinion.

PREPARATION TIME
00 : 00 : 15

RESPONSE TIME
00 : 01 : 00

Question 11: Express an Opinion

答題範例

 **Question 11**

> *This statement is fundamentally incorrect.*
>
> There is no doubt that technology has improved the quality of life.
>
> Life now is easier and safer, and it's thanks to technology.
>
> Can you imagine our lives without electricity?
>
> What about the Internet and computers? Cars and planes?
>
> Can you imagine traveling for hundreds of kilometers on a donkey or on a camel?
>
> Without technology, our lives would be harder, slower and less enjoyable.
>
> On the other hand, we cannot deny that technology has caused many problems.
>
> Pollution and health problems due to the speed of life have resulted from technology.
>
> *However, these problems are correctable by more advanced technologies.*
>
> For example, health problems are caused by pollution.
>
> Technology allows us to develop treatments and eliminate the source.
>
> Millions of people would die every year if not for pesticides.
>
> Crops would be destroyed and diseases would spread.
>
> As insects develop different defenses—technology has to constantly keep up.
>
> In conclusion, though technology may cause many problems, the benefits of
>   technology undoubtedly overcome its drawbacks.
>
> There are real problems that can occur due to technology.
>
> But these problems are manageable by more advanced technologies.

GO ON TO THE NEXT PAGE.

NO TEST MATERIAL ON THIS PAGE

New TOEIC Writing Test

Questions 1-5: Write a Sentence Based on a Picture

Question 1

Directions: Write ONE sentence based on the picture using the TWO words or phrases under it. You may change the forms of the words and you may use them in any order.

man / engine

答題範例：**The man is working on the engine.**

GO ON TO THE NEXT PAGE.

Questions 1-5: Write a Sentence Based on a Picture

Question 2

Directions: Write ONE sentence based on the picture using the TWO words or phrases under it. You may change the forms of the words and you may use them in any order.

lay / brick

答題範例：**The man is laying bricks.**

Questions 1-5: Write a Sentence Based on a Picture

Question 3

Directions: Write ONE sentence based on the picture using the TWO words or phrases under it. You may change the forms of the words and you may use them in any order.

tourist / bus

答題範例：**Some tourists are boarding the bus.**

GO ON TO THE NEXT PAGE.

Questions 1-5: Write a Sentence Based on a Picture

Question 4

Directions: Write ONE sentence based on the picture using the TWO words or phrases under it. You may change the forms of the words and you may use them in any order.

store / computer

答題範例：**The men are in a store that sells computers.**

Questions 1-5: Write a Sentence Based on a Picture

Question 5

Directions: Write ONE sentence based on the picture using the TWO words or phrases under it. You may change the forms of the words and you may use them in any order.

restroom / clean

答題範例：**The woman is cleaning the restroom.**

GO ON TO THE NEXT PAGE.

Questions 6-7: Respond to a written request

Question 6

Directions: Read the e-mail below.

From: Ted North <t_north@jjventures.com>
To: Andy Green <a_green@jjventures.com>
Subject: URGENT! Please Open Immediately!
Date: October 12

Andy,

As you know, I arrived in Dallas to meet the clients this morning. However, the airline lost my luggage, which contained the samples for the meeting tomorrow. I just got off the phone with a guy from the airline; they've located my luggage—it got sent to Seattle. Unfortunately, they say it could be anywhere from 1-3 days before it's returned to me. That isn't going to work for us. I need those product samples to show the client; otherwise, we might as well cancel the meeting. Is there anything you could do on your end to help?

Thanks in advance,

Ted North
Lead Sales Representative, Southwest Region
JJ Ventures, Inc.

Directions: Write back to Ted North as Andy Green. Acknowledge and offer ONE solution to his problem.

Questions 6-7: Respond to a written request

答題範例

Question 6

Ted,

I'm sorry to hear about your luggage. At least the airline has located your suitcase. Since it's not possible to determine when your luggage will be found and returned, I've sent product samples by overnight shipping. That way, you will not have to go empty-handed to tomorrow's meeting with the clients. There are five samples of each product as well as complete descriptions. I sent the items by NSFW Overnight to your hotel. The package will be delivered by 8:30 a.m. so that you are sure to have product samples to show when you speak at the 10:00 a.m. meeting in Dallas.

Good luck,

Allen Green
J.J. Ventures, Inc.

GO ON TO THE NEXT PAGE.

Questions 6-7: Respond to a written request

Question 7

Directions: Read the e-mail below.

From: Moishe Fields <moishe@rippers.com>
To: Digger Fox <digger@remco.com>
Date: May 4
Subject: REMCO-18-0219 Shipment

Dear Mr. Fox,

The box containing shipment REMCO-18-0219 arrived today and it included an item we had not ordered: a guitar interface. I spotted this error immediately and checked the invoice. However, it indicates that we have been charged the full amount of this item. We request the $108 difference to be refunded. I assume that you would like the interface to be sent back to you. Your website indicates that defective products and incorrect items can be returned free of charge, but no details are provided regarding your shipping preferences. Please tell me how I should proceed.

Regards,

Moishe Fields

Ripper's Music

Directions: Reply to Mr. Fields as Digger Fox, a sales manager from REMCO Industries. Apologize for the mistake and inform Mr. Fields that you will refund his money, and give him TWO shipping options to return the item.

Questions 6-7: Respond to a written request

答題範例

Question 7

Mr. Fields,

I sincerely apologize for the inconvenience of our mistake. Of course, I will refund your money promptly. As for returning the guitar interface, I can offer two options. First, you can return it by post, free of charge. Simply tell the clerk to send it Cash on Delivery (C.O.D.). Second, I could arrange for one of our own delivery drivers to retrieve the item from your store whenever it's convenient for you.

Please let me know which option is preferable to you.

Sincerely,
Digger Fox
REMCO Industries

GO ON TO THE NEXT PAGE.

Questions 8: Write an opinion essay

Question 8

Directions: Read the question below. You have 30 minutes to plan, write, and revise your essay. Typically, an effective response will contain a minimum of 300 words.

Should governments spend more money on improving roads and highways, or should governments spend more money on improving public transportation (buses, trains, subways)? Why? Use specific reasons and details to develop your essay.

Questions 8: Write an opinion essay

答題範例

Question 8

In my opinion, upgrading the public transportation system brings more advantages.

First, let's analyze why improving roads and highways is not a good option. As we all know, the number of cars has risen tremendously in the last few decades. Building roads does not solve the problem of traffic jams but encourages more and more people to use their own cars instead of buses and subways. Moreover, it is very expensive to invest in roads and highways projects, and these projects often cause more problems. When roads or highways are being repaired, construction companies have to close them and people have to use other streets. This can cause a street to be overcrowded with cars; therefore, a lot of people will be stuck in traffic jams. The average commuter wastes about one week each year in traffic jams. Traffic jams make the economy lose a lot of money each year. Cars in traffic jams cannot move, but they continue to emit harmful smoke, which will make the global warming issue more severe.

Another reason why upgrading public transit services is preferable is that it alleviates environmental problems. If we have good public transportation, more and more people will use buses or subways instead of using cars. The amount of traffic will decrease; therefore, there will be less harmful smoke, the main cause of air pollution and global warming, in the air. Furthermore, we have to know that governments work for the people. Many people in the middle and lower classes, who account for a large portion of the population, use public transportation because the cost is low. If we build more roads, only people in the upper class can benefit from this. A good government is a government that serves all people, not only a small group of wealthy individuals. If all people use buses or subways, they will develop a sense of community.

Those are the reasons why I think governments should concentrate on improving public transportation. I use buses as much as I can. If we all use buses or subways, this world will be a better world.

TOEIC 練習測驗 答案紙

LISTENING SECTION

Part 1

No.	ANSWER
1	A B C D
2	A B C D
3	A B C D
4	A B C D
5	A B C D
6	A B C D
7	A B C D
8	A B C D
9	A B C D
10	A B C D

Part 2

No.	ANSWER
11	A B C
12	A B C
13	A B C
14	A B C
15	A B C
16	A B C
17	A B C
18	A B C
19	A B C
20	A B C
21	A B C
22	A B C
23	A B C
24	A B C
25	A B C
26	A B C
27	A B C
28	A B C
29	A B C
30	A B C

Part 3

No.	ANSWER
31	A B C D
32	A B C D
33	A B C D
34	A B C D
35	A B C D
36	A B C D
37	A B C D
38	A B C D
39	A B C D
40	A B C D
41	A B C D
42	A B C D
43	A B C D
44	A B C D
45	A B C D
46	A B C D
47	A B C D
48	A B C D
49	A B C D
50	A B C D
51	A B C D
52	A B C D
53	A B C D
54	A B C D
55	A B C D
56	A B C D
57	A B C D
58	A B C D
59	A B C D
60	A B C D
61	A B C D
62	A B C D
63	A B C D
64	A B C D
65	A B C D
66	A B C D
67	A B C D
68	A B C D
69	A B C D
70	A B C D

Part 4

No.	ANSWER
71	A B C D
72	A B C D
73	A B C D
74	A B C D
75	A B C D
76	A B C D
77	A B C D
78	A B C D
79	A B C D
80	A B C D
81	A B C D
82	A B C D
83	A B C D
84	A B C D
85	A B C D
86	A B C D
87	A B C D
88	A B C D
89	A B C D
90	A B C D
91	A B C D
92	A B C D
93	A B C D
94	A B C D
95	A B C D
96	A B C D
97	A B C D
98	A B C D
99	A B C D
100	A B C D

READING SECTION

Part 5

No.	ANSWER
101	A B C D
102	A B C D
103	A B C D
104	A B C D
105	A B C D
106	A B C D
107	A B C D
108	A B C D
109	A B C D
110	A B C D
111	A B C D
112	A B C D
113	A B C D
114	A B C D
115	A B C D
116	A B C D
117	A B C D
118	A B C D
119	A B C D
120	A B C D
121	A B C D
122	A B C D
123	A B C D
124	A B C D
125	A B C D
126	A B C D
127	A B C D
128	A B C D
129	A B C D
130	A B C D

Part 6

No.	ANSWER
131	A B C D
132	A B C D
133	A B C D
134	A B C D
135	A B C D
136	A B C D
137	A B C D
138	A B C D
139	A B C D
140	A B C D
141	A B C D
142	A B C D
143	A B C D
144	A B C D
145	A B C D
146	A B C D
147	A B C D
148	A B C D
149	A B C D
150	A B C D

Part 7

No.	ANSWER
151	A B C D
152	A B C D
153	A B C D
154	A B C D
155	A B C D
156	A B C D
157	A B C D
158	A B C D
159	A B C D
160	A B C D
161	A B C D
162	A B C D
163	A B C D
164	A B C D
165	A B C D
166	A B C D
167	A B C D
168	A B C D
169	A B C D
170	A B C D
171	A B C D
172	A B C D
173	A B C D
174	A B C D
175	A B C D
176	A B C D
177	A B C D
178	A B C D
179	A B C D
180	A B C D
181	A B C D
182	A B C D
183	A B C D
184	A B C D
185	A B C D
186	A B C D
187	A B C D
188	A B C D
189	A B C D
190	A B C D
191	A B C D
192	A B C D
193	A B C D
194	A B C D
195	A B C D
196	A B C D
197	A B C D
198	A B C D
199	A B C D
200	A B C D